T0128865

Other Books by Rae D'Arcy

Hoof Beats
Horse Power

MAGIC HORSES

By

Rae D'Arcy

 www.trafford.com

North America & international
toll-free: 1 888 232 4444 (USA & Canada)
fax: 812 355 4082

To my favorite horse child, Rylynn

CHAPTER ONE

I stood in the midst of my dream with the April sun shining on my face. My dream surrounded me in all its glory; it was the result of years of work and sacrifice. Those bygone years should have been the best of my life. I had spent them all working for this. Here it was at last, and all I could feel was anger.

The moving van had just negotiated the turn from my long lane onto the main road, its rumble deepening as the driver accelerated, shifted, and accelerated again. I pivoted and surveyed my kingdom, including the hay barn, the stables, the fenced pastures, and the fields beyond. The old farmhouse had extensions added, the interior remodeled, and new vinyl siding coated its outer walls. There was a new three-car garage topped with a furnished apartment and outbuildings that still needed to be painted. I had worked so hard for it, and now that I had it, my overweight, aching body chided that I would not be able to enjoy it.

I turned, hobbled toward the hay barn and, opened wide the sliding door on its track. It was just a pole building with a plank floor covered in skids that would keep the hay dry. Three loads of grass hay would arrive tomorrow and would take most of the day to fill half of the building. The other half would be partially filled with oat straw the following week. Hopefully, this would be the only year I'd have to purchase these commodities. I had high hopes that my farm would be self-sufficient by next spring.

It was a warm day, so I left the door open to air out the building. I turned toward the stables. The newly laid, fine gravel made walking harder and exacerbated the pain in my arthritic knees and back. The sliding doors were already open, enticing the musty smell, mold, and dust from yesterday's cleaning to ride away on the occasional breeze. The tractor and manure spreader were still parked at the lower end of the cemented aisle. I was pleased that the previous owners had put in good, solid stalls. There were twelve in all. If I ever needed to, I could lease out a few.

I couldn't help but stand just outside what would be the grain room at the head of the aisle to visualize the horses that would stand at their stall guards, looking my way expectantly. I longed for the smells of horse, hay, and grain to fill the air. Someday, and soon I hoped, many of these stalls would be occupied.

I struggled to the huge arena next. Each span of beams was reinforced with two-by-fours forming triangles across the vaulted ceiling to provide extraordinary strength. No amount of snow would collapse that roof. I would have guaranteed year-round riding.

I snorted in disgust. *I've been on my feet too long*, I mused. It was affecting my brain. My lower back was screaming in pain, and I was starting to grit my teeth. If I couldn't do a little work, how would I be able to ride? I sat in a chair in an enclosed observation area to let the discomfort abate and then tried to walk as though no pain dogged my steps all the way to the house.

I took pleasure in the plush carpeting throughout the house as well as the color schemes overflowing from one room into the next, leading me from one garden of hues and tones to another. I was a bit sad that it wasn't cooler so I could light a fire in the pit in the great room or even the fireplace in the living room. I consoled myself that there might yet be a cool spell for creating an entrancing fire. My analytic mind questioned, *What will you do with such cozy comforts in such a large house all alone?*

I can entertain, I countered.

Who, pray tell? You have no friends.

I stood stunned with that realization, and then it shook my insides to be so alone. My buildings were still empty. The house was newly occupied by me and did not quite feel like home. Today was my first day of retirement. What do I do with myself? There was no one to call and no one to come celebrate with. A partially painted canvas was on the easel, but I wasn't in the mood to paint or write. I had been waiting for this point in time for years. Here it was at last, and I felt powerless to grasp it. I had never needed people before. They had never fit into my dream. Why did I think I needed them now? Because that was an awful lot to not share.

Easy does it, I crooned to myself. *You knew it would take time to shift gears. Enjoy now. You have plenty of time. Learn to walk slowly and smell the flowers again.*

I walked through the newly added part of the house that had been attached to the rear of the original farmhouse. The great room was the middle portion beneath the peaked roof. Sticking out the west side of that was an exercise room with large windows facing the back acres. I felt light-headed as I realized that it was created for someone who expected to spend a lot of time alone. Past the equipment and into a smaller room was a small pool with flowing current big enough for one. It had two walls of windows, one to the west and the other also facing the backyard, which was north. On the east of the great room was a greenhouse where I hoped to grow vegetables for the table during the winter months. As a buffer between the greenhouse and the great room was a small washroom where I could wash the vegetables and rinse the soil from my hands and leave my work boots so I didn't track unnecessary dirt into the house.

French doors led off the great room onto a patio and about an acre of land surrounded by a four-foot chain-link fence. I paused to admire the huge planters on the patio containing magnolia and yew and then shifted my gaze to the yard beyond, where spaced about were white dogwood, redbud, and crab apple trees. There were lilac bushes, ornamental grasses, and areas of sedum or ivy as ground cover. In spots of shade or full sun, benches of wrought iron, redwood, or resin sat at convenient spots for watching the birds that utilized what I had painstakingly provided for them, thinking natural would be better than feeders. I made my way to the first redwood, which was actually a swing, to try to shift gears by gazing at the spring beauty.

Along the side edges of the yard, on the other side of the fence, were shrubs that would provide shelter as well as seeds or berries for the wintering birds, hopefully, so they would leave my own blackberries and cherries alone, which were beyond the back fence, just before the orchard of apples, peaches, pears, and red plums.

I gently pushed off to set the swing into motion and watched the birds madly building nests or feeding their first brood of young. Two shepherd hooks stood a short distance away, holding suet cages. I smiled at the "natural" rule already broken. I'd provide for them only in early spring and winter, I reasoned. They'd provide lots of energy for the frantic, aerial activity all around me. The birds were frightened of my nearness, scowling and scolding from perches near and far before flying away to look for other sources of food. I expected their reaction but hoped that at a near-future point in time, my presence wouldn't frighten them, that they would see me as a benefactor, and that they would know that I had planted the serviceberry, verbena, and burning bush, pampas grass, and yarrow for their benefit.

I thought I saw a flash of blue a half acre away near the bluebird box and rued the fact that I had not brought my field glasses. I refused to go get them. It was enough knowing the box would be used.

I closed my eyes and lifted my face to the sun. With the birds singing backup, I let the warmth coax thoughts of my life's journey into my mind. Tears immediately slid from beneath closed lids as I thought of my failed marriage to Daniel. Now it seemed so wrong that I withheld any extra money I had made as a nurse. My dream had been forever in my mind. I had picked up overtime whenever I could and put the financial gain back into interest-bearing CDs. I refused to move to a fancier house, buy adult toys, or need children to complete me. I paid my fair share of expenses, encouraged Dan to explore his interests with his own paycheck, went on modest vacations, and indulged in books on horse care and training. I even took some riding lessons. I took painting lessons and creative writing classes. I did everything to prepare for this moment in time . . . alone.

I wasn't, however, a shopper. I wore clothes until they were unusable. I limited eating out and didn't buy music or movies. I didn't color or perm my hair and didn't waste money on jewelry. When Dan wanted a divorce, it was almost a relief. He felt that I was investing more in my dream than in our relationship. I had to admit the validity of that. I let him buy out my half of the house, and I moved to a small apartment so I could save monies that would have been sucked away for upkeep and repairs. I found a second job. For years, I didn't notice I was alone. There was, after all, interaction with the people at my jobs. When I did notice, I simply worked harder to make my dream come true.

I opened my tear-filled eyes and saw my yard covered in rainbows. I had to smile at the fairylike effect. I blinked; the tears slid down my cheeks, and my yard looked real again. For a moment, I wondered if I would do it differently if given the chance. Most likely not, I conceded. *There's no use shedding tears over it*, I chided myself. But there was no one to share it with.

You aren't ready to share, said the voice in my head that normally carried on conversations with me.

I felt a pain in my chest at about the same location as my heart. To think I was so immature as to be unable to share.

Not unable. Just not ready, the mental voice clarified.

What's the difference? I wondered. *It still boils down to not sharing.*

There's a difference. You have to have the right people to share it with, someone who will appreciate it and the sacrifice it took to get it.

I closed my eyes, the better to feel the afternoon sun on my face and to relax my shoulders. It seemed but an instant later that a chill made me shiver, and I opened my eyes again. I was still upright. The control I wielded over myself for years still held sway. The sun was reaching out for the western horizon, casually glancing back at a vanishing day. Huge dark thunderclouds hung overhead. It smelled of rain unshed.

I hobbled to the hay barn and slid the door shut to bar the coming dampness from reentering. As I hurried to close the doors at either end of the stable row, I looked down the lane, hoping a neighbor was coming with a pie or cookies or just a few words of welcome to the area. I was only halfway to the house before the clouds released their burden in a downpour of fat, heavy drops reflecting my sadness that there was no welcome, just an empty lane.

I locked the door of the mudroom behind me, stripped from my soaked clothes and threw them into the washer, and slid into a terry robe hanging by the machine. As I climbed the stairs, I wondered how I could have forgotten to prepare to have people in my retirement. All my preparation was in expecting to be alone—writing, painting, solitary endeavors.

Passing the bathroom, I flicked on the switch to the heating elements in the floor. I lit votive candles along the edge of the tub and started the water running, adding lavender scent. By the time I returned with gown, slippers, and plush robe, the thick maize-colored carpet was warm to the soles of my bare feet. For a moment, I stood savoring the luxurious feeling and then crawled into the calming, hot, suds-covered water.

As the liquid heat coaxed the tension from my muscles, I had a moment of guilt. I had been raised with the erroneous idea that money and luxury were the root of all evil, but my mind reminded me that it was the love of money that was the evil. My money would be the means to help unfortunate horses. I had worked hard and sacrificed much to prepare for that goal. I let my body melt and become putty. *Ready for the potter's hand*, I mused.

I dozed again and awoke to flickering flames as the only light. I felt heavy with relaxation as I emerged from the cooled water. The towel, slippers, and robe were warm from lying on the warmed carpet. I walked to the bedroom and sat in an armchair to listen to the silence echo throughout the house and watch the rain. It seemed that Mother Nature was crying. Suddenly tears were streaming down my face as well, and I didn't really understand why.

Oh, for pity's sake, I scolded. *Why are you sad?*

I'm worried about the rain ruining the loads of hay that will be arriving in the morning, I lied as though it were possible to lie to myself.

Don't worry until you have something to worry about, I answered, not at all taken in by my lie.

What a wasted day, I countered.

You enjoyed it, I retorted. *Take it easy; take your time; enjoy the transition. Even if you sleep the first month, your body and mind probably need it after forty-some years of working sixty-plus hours a week.*

Still to counter any future bouts of sadness, I determined to create a blessings list for all I had to be thankful for and to recite it anytime I felt sadness approaching.

It was a good first day of retirement.

CHAPTER TWO

I was out of bed as the sun peeked over the rim of the earth. I was relieved to see a clear sky. I had phone calls I wanted to make before the hay trucks rolled in. One was to the Humane Society for Hoofed Animals. Another was to Equine Angels Rescue. I wanted them both to know I was available to foster rescued horses. During the phone calls, they both said they'd send someone to inspect my place for suitability within the next month. I was disappointed that it would take that long.

I got a big pot of chili cooking using spicy chili beans and chili powder. I preferred a more bland recipe, but Frank Todd said the workers coming to unload the hay were migrant workers from south of the border. I whipped together a large batch of corn bread as well and made up platters of ham and roast beef sandwiches. While everything was cooking, I got on the Internet to look for a horse or two for myself.

The first tractor rolled in at ten, followed by a pickup truck full of short brown men and one young woman. They sprang from the truck bed and scurried into the hay barn. Frank waved to me from the tractor, then neatly backed the wagon into the hay barn, let a worker unhitch, and left. I couldn't believe how no one needed to direct them. They seemed to know where the hay barn was and assumed they needed no permission to open the doors, offered guidance to Frank as he backed the trailer, and knew which side of the building to start stacking the bales. They swarmed like a hive of honeybees, their chatter creating a hum.

Just as they finished unloading the first trailer, a tractor pulling a slanted conveyor drove down the lane, followed closely by another load of hay. The Mexicans pushed and pulled the first emptied trailer out of the hay barn. Frank backed the conveyor into the building. As someone adjusted its height, someone else unhitched it. A few others unloaded a generator that would power the conveyor. Frank pulled away, and the next hay wagon was aligned to the conveyor. It was all accomplished within a matter of minutes. The team ran as a well-oiled machine. Immediately the bales were sliding up the conveyor, and workers continued stacking them in a neat, alternating pattern with a slight space between the bales to allow airflow.

I called to Frank. "Have you a moment to help me bring out a couple picnic tables from the garage?"

"Sure."

I gritted my teeth as I carried my end of the tables as well as a huge trash can for the waste. "That was close timing, Frank. Be sure to give them time for a meal after they're done with this load."

"I will. By the way, Jillian, have you noticed the young couple?"

"Not specifically. The whole group works so well together, although I did notice a young woman was among them. She's coupled with which man?"

"The one in dark-green work pants. That's Sergio. He put in your oat crop. Elena is his wife. They have two well-behaved children: Joaquin and Milagro. They've just gotten their citizenship. You said you needed workers. Sergio has done wonderful at my place. He's a good worker."

"The apartment over the garage is only a one bedroom. And I'm not sure about children running around."

"Compared to what they're living in now, that will seem like a palace. And believe me, the children are well controlled. I think you'll be amazed."

"How old are the children?"

"Four and five. The girl will start preschool, and the boy kindergarten this fall. And I believe Elena is going to attend LPN school starting in June."

"Who'll take care of the children?"

"They have an old woman living with them that cares for them. That's an interesting story too. Maybe they'll share it with you sometime."

"Well, if you're recommending them, I'll hire them."

Frank clapped his hands. "Wonderful. I'll help move them in tonight after work. About seven?"

"That's fine. The apartment has the basics—a double bed, bureau, couch, kitchen appliances, table, and chairs."

"They'll make do. Is the salary still what you told me last week?"

"It is."

Frank left with a smile on his face. He had a big heart and was helping interested migrants get their citizenship. Each time he found permanent employment for one of his workers, he was ecstatic. Those who hired his workers found themselves part of a system enabling people to better themselves. Frank had assured me that they would be here only as long as it took them to get an education for themselves, and they could move on to better jobs. I knew that after Elena got an LPN job, she would pay for Sergio to get an education. And then they would be gone, and Frank would recommend others to help on my farm. But it could be several years before Elena and Sergio were at that point. Frank had also assured me that they would not neglect their work while getting their education.

I felt a spark of hope at having others around as I started carrying out paper bowls, napkins, cups, and plasticware. I brought out three two-gallon buckets of hot water with washcloths and towels. As they were washing the hay from their hot, tired bodies, I made another trip into the house to carry out the large pot of chili, a tray of corn bread, and the platters of stacked sandwiches. Sergio and Elena scrambled to help me. They made eye contact, and I saw the hope shining in the dark depths. I filled cups with sweet cold water from the hose. Elena ladled chili into bowls, making sure I knew one was for me. Sergio scooped large pieces of corn bread onto small paper plates and passed them around.

The chatter and laughter drifted on the breeze like dandelion seed heads between hands grabbing for sandwiches and plasticware and then fell silent while mouths were busy with eating. I saw quick hands surreptitiously wrap sandwiches in napkins and stuff them into pockets. When they were satisfied, they moved to the cool grass to smoke and let the food settle in their stomachs.

At first, I was appalled that they would steal. After all, I was not required to provide the meal. And then I thought their road must be a hard one on such low pay. I went into the house to get plastic grocery bags, ziplock sandwich bags, and plastic deli containers. I went back out and filled the leftovers in the containers and sat them on top of the grocery bags.

"Help yourselves to anything you want to take home with you," I said and then began to carry empty pots and platters back in, with the young couple jumping up to help, hoping to make a good impression. "So I hear you want a job here?"

"I want a job, *si*. I will work hard for you."

"I can do housework too," added Elena nervously.

"I thought you were going to school?"

"Si, but I can clean before or after classes."

"I would want you to do well in your classes."

"Perhaps I could exchange cleaning for some tutoring, but only if you have time." She gave a small hopeful smile. "You were a nurse, si?"

I smiled back. "Yes, I was a nurse. Maybe we can work something out."

"Gracias. We will work very hard for you."

"Who will babysit while you are working or going to classes?"

"The children must learn to work also. And we also have Wee Shee."

"Who is Wee Shee?"

"She is from the old country. She has taken care of the children since they were born. It is an honor for us to have her share her age wisdom with us and to teach the children this wisdom. It is an important part of their education."

"You know the apartment has only one bedroom, don't you?"

"Si" was all she said as though nothing else needed to be said.

It was seven o'clock on the dot when a rusted old dodge ram pulled close to the stairs leading up to the apartment over the garage. Everyone jumped out and grabbed something to carry up the steps. Even the two small children and a birdlike tiny old woman with terra-cotta skin and long straight black hair carried boxes. No sooner had they had everything off the truck than Frank pulled in with his truck and carried bigger items. I watched closely and saw two dressers, a mirrored bureau, a tall bookcase, and mattresses carried up the steps by Sergio and his mentor.

When the last piece was carried up the stairs, I walked over to take a plate of cookies and to be sure that they found the keys hanging on the key holder just inside the door.

"Gracias," Elena thanked me for the cookies and then introduced me to the old woman. "This is Wheeeesheeee." She made the sound of wind through the trees. "But we shorten it to Wee Shee for ease. Or you can just call her Wind."

"Welcome, Wee Shee."

The old woman answered nothing. She just stared at me with her black eyes. I found it disconcerting. Did she not speak or understand English? Or maybe she thought it beneath her to speak to a gringo.

I turned back to Elena. "Well, I hope you'll be comfortable here."

Frank was smiling at me. It gave me a warm feeling, not only that I'd be helping this small family trying to better themselves, but that I had pleased Frank as well. I made a mental note that Frank and his wife, Gloria, might be new friends I could cultivate. I could start by becoming a part of their system of helping the less fortunate attain their dreams.

CHAPTER THREE

I thought I was an early riser, but as I got my cup of coffee and stood at the kitchen sink being thankful for another day of sunshine, I saw Elena and the chi\ldren dressed in sweaters against the chill, all pulling early-season weeds from around the spent daffodils, blooming tulips, lupine, and sprouting lilies. Elena was showing Milagro how to bend the daffodil leaves over and wrap one leaf around the others to hold them in place. She then began to hoe the soil loose. Bags of mulch were stacked nearby. The tractor was parked by the garage. The manure spreader had been replaced by a trailer. Sergio was loading one-by-six-inch planks and a can of white paint. He called to Joaquin, who, glad to be released from the women's work, ran to join his father. They drove slowly. Joaquin was on his father's lap, his hands on the steering wheel alongside his father's, and their hair was blowing the same way in the breeze like a choreographed dance.

I assumed they were going to repair the rails on the fence along the property frontage. There were a few slats missing. I was extremely pleased that Sergio was getting started on the to-do list that I had made and hung just inside the garage door before I had even hired him. I was prepared. The boards were stacked against the garage wall, and the cans of paint were on the shelf. How lucky I was that I had such self-motivated people on my payroll.

With a start, I saw Wee Shee standing by the flower bed, looking at me. I was sure she had not been there originally. I suddenly felt guilty watching others do the work. What could I set my hand to so as not to feel like a feudal lord? I knew I was being silly as I had, after all, hired them to do the work.

Still, I scurried to my pool and swam until I was in danger of sinking to the bottom like a definned shark. I had to cling to the side of the pool, breathing heavy, letting the current float my rubbery legs out behind me until I felt steady enough to get dressed and go to my study. I booted up the computer and spent an hour typing whatever came to mind, hoping that a few seeds of ideas would sprout into a novel.

Promptly at ten o'clock, Elena knocked at the door. I was dismayed to see she had brought Milagro with her, but I said nothing. I showed her where the cleaning supplies were and gave her a suggestion on how often I wanted baseboards and walls done. The surface things could be done every couple of days. I couldn't help but notice that Milagro was quiet and very attentive.

It was a cool day. I put my hands in the pockets of my hoodie as I trudged across the gravel toward the stables and felt my knees scream in arthritic pain. That was when I saw Joaquin coming down the lane. He was carrying a paint can in his right hand and a paintbrush in his left. He listed to the right and wobbled back to the left. His left arm stuck out and flailed to and fro, sending sprinkles of white paint flying through the air as his small body accommodated the heavy paint can on the other side. I was appalled at the amount of paint he had on himself and that his father had left him the chore of returning the paint supplies.

I heard the guttural roar of the rototiller and saw Sergio starting to turn the soil in the garden area. My jaw dropped. Surely Joaquin hadn't done the painting also? My first impulse was to check what kind of a job a five-year-old could have done, but I caught myself and continued to the stable. I would check the work when I went out for an errand.

I got a broom and swept the bristles over the bars between the stalls to remove cobwebs and swept the concrete aisle again. I peeked out a stall window and saw Joaquin walking in front of his father, holding on to the bucking rototiller. He had a big grin on his face as he stumbled over the upturned earth. It bothered me that one so young was attempting to do grown-up work.

Again I wondered if I should intervene. But then I knew the value being part of the team would have on them. Okay then. Let them learn to work, but I was determined to provide something they could enjoy—a jungle gym, a small pool, maybe even a trampoline.

That was when I saw Wee Shee standing at the corner of the garage, looking at me. I jumped back, startled that her eyes seemed so black and penetrating even from that distance. Surely she couldn't see me in the stall window from that far away. And yet it surely seemed she could. *And why was she watching me so closely?* I wondered.

I was sweating from the ache in my back as well as from the exertion of swinging and pushing the broom. I put it away and went to the house for my binoculars and journal. I thought I'd smile and say good day to Wee Shee to ease the tension I felt under her scrutiny, but she was nowhere to be seen. I passed Milagro sitting in the new gravel, trying to see how many stones she could pile atop one another. I had the unkind thought that Wee Shee wasn't much of a babysitter to leave her charge alone like that.

I was about to speak to the little girl when she looked up and waved toward their apartment above the garage. I felt a chill. I couldn't help turning to look, expecting to see Wee Shee staring out a window. Instead, I saw a snowy owl sitting on the peak. Milagro got up and ran toward it, disappearing around the side of the building as it took flight down the length of my acre of yard. I felt a keen disappointment that the child had scared it away.

I didn't think snowies were this far south. I added the bird guide to my other paraphernalia and went to sit on the redwood swing. Using the field glasses, I scanned the treetops, hoping to spot the white owl. I panned back and forth, bringing the search a little lower with each pass until Milagro was in my sights. She was squatting, her knees close to her chest, her arms straight at her sides, turning her head from side to side and winking one dark eye, looking ever so much like a fledgling owl.

I heard clapping. I dropped the binoculars to hang from their strap around my neck and saw Wee Shee a few feet from Milagro. They ignored me as, hand in hand, they walked back to the garage; and I was left with goose bumps not caused by the lively, cool breeze.

CHAPTER FOUR

I had just gotten a shower after working out when the phone rang.

"Jillian Debaum?"

"Speaking."

"This is Grace Armstead with the Equine Angels Rescue. Are you prepared to take in a horse in need of rescuing?

"Well, my straw hasn't arrived yet, and no one has been out to inspect the premises."

"We're pretty desperate for help."

"I could go to the feedstore for some straw. What have you got?"

"An abandoned herd of Thoroughbred broodmares across the state line. Aborted foals. Some horses barely standing. Can you help?"

"Sure. I have a two-horse trailer, but I could make two trips if need be."

"Do you have a fax machine?"

"Yes."

"Give me the number. I'll fax the directions."

I quickly packed a lunch with a thermos of hot coffee, threw some extra clothes in a duffel bag, just in case, and headed for the truck, yelling for Sergio along the way. I gave him money to go to the feedstore for straw and senior feed. As he helped me hitch the trailer and check the lights and turn signals, I told him where I was going. I put hay in the hay nets inside the trailer, filled the water buckets about two-thirds full of water, and added a ten-inch piece of two-by-four board to keep it from sloshing. I went back to the house for the faxed instructions, and I was on my way.

It was another beautiful morning—sunny, with just a bit of coolness in the air. It was a perfect day for hauling. Not too hot, not too cool. I wanted to watch the countryside slide by, but I had to keep checking the directions and watch for mileage and landmarks. I didn't want to waste time by getting lost. I was determined to make two trips.

It took me an hour and a half to get to the state line and another twenty minutes to find the abandoned farm. There were other trailers arriving, many parked and a few leaving. It made me wonder if there would be any horses left for me. But it turned out that many vehicles were hauling nothing but spectators. They stood at the fence shaking heads and mumbling about the atrocious sight. Others milled about the huge herd, picking and choosing, asking names, injuries, and chances of survival. Then there were the ones with bandannas over their noses trying to clear the area of aborted foals and mares and trying to follow the dead bodies of their babies being hauled away. I could only stare at the horrible scene.

A bearded man with a clipboard in his hand and weariness on his face came toward me. "You are who?"

"Jillian Debaum. They called me this morning."

"Have a preference of color?" His tiredness rippled in his voice, and I thought I heard some scorn. "Most of them are bays. Here's a list of their names. They have a tag on their halter with a number that corresponds to their jockey club name. See? Number one is Bird in the Willows. The check mark means she's gone. She was in pretty good shape and not hard to catch with a handful of hay."

The stench was overwhelming. I had to put my hand over my nose and mouth for a moment to filter the air I was taking in. "I'll take whichever ones we can get into my trailer."

"Quite a few aren't going to make it, even if they can make it into a trailer." He said, watching for my reaction.

"Well, they all deserve a chance even if it's just to feel warm and fed their last days . . . or hours," I growled at him.

I saw something flicker in his brown eyes as he looked at me a second longer. I held his gaze defiantly and thought I saw one corner of his mustached lip twitch. Was he laughing at my sentimentality?

"Do you have leads?"

"Yep," I answered, softening my tone. I grabbed the two from the front seat.

We walked among the other people with clipboards helping a few other rescuers pick the horses of their choice. There were small piles of hay and buckets of water here and there. Mares showing ribs and hip bones stood munching, their watery eyes watching the roving people. Some moved away as people approached as though fearing what new horror awaited them with the new faces.

We were passing a huge gray mare standing over the dried remains of the carcass of an aborted foal. I guessed it was hers. There wasn't much left of her either. Her head hung almost to the ground as though it was too heavy to lift. I thought I saw her sway. My stomach rolled, and tears came to my eyes. I noticed there was no hay or water near her. I walked to her and placed my hand gently on her back. There was no response, no flick of ears, no eye rolled in fear, no curiosity to know where the touch came from, no quiver to rid her dirty hide of the fly my soft touch could have been. I made a gentle scratching on her withers.

"She isn't going to make it," he repeated. "I doubt she has the strength to walk into a trailer. Save your efforts for one that has a chance."

I wheeled toward him. I bit my lips to keep from saying something I might regret, but I must have been shooting daggers from my eyes because he literally took a step back. I took a deep breath and said, "Sorry. It's not your fault. Let's find me a couple horses."

Some of the mares were stronger and moved quickly away from us. "They were the strongest," my escort explained. "Pushed the others away from whatever food and water was available."

I reached for the halter of another gray just as another woman approached.

"I was heading for this horse," she whined. "I specifically wanted a gray."

I threw both my hands in the air. "She's all yours." As I turned to see what other horse was nearby, my elbow bumped against an equine head near my back. "Oops. Sorry, sweetie. I didn't see you."

She was huge and black. My bump hardly startled her, or else she just didn't have the strength to react.

"She's been making her way toward you since you petted the gray that's gonna die." He kept his eyes on his clipboard so as not to meet mine.

"What's the number on her tag?"

"Twenty." He flipped a page of his list. "Her name is Hag of the Bog. Want her?"

"Yep. Let's get her loaded."

"Go ahead. Walk her nice and slow. Tell me what else you want. I'll try to get her in line for loading."

"Get whatever can make it to the trailer. Preferably whatever might not be wanted by anyone else."

I wanted to groan about the pain in my back and knees, but I forced my mind into thinking of what kind of call name I could make out of Hag of the Bog. I didn't like Haggie, Boggie, Habbie, Hoggie, or Hobbie. But that was pretty close to Hobbit, and that was what I settled on. Halfway to the trailer, Hobbit had to stop for a rest. I leaned over, hands on my knees to ease my own pain. We continued on, and she loaded calmly. I heard her heave a sigh as she smelled and then tugged at the hay in the net.

I could see the clipboard man making his way slowly with another horse. I got a handful of sweet-smelling grass hay from the other net and a one-gallon ice cream bucket from behind the truck seat, filled it with water, and took it to the gray. I figured she was too weak to pick her head up over the edge of a regular water bucket, and if she did, she might have drowned, not being able to hold her head up to keep her nose out of the water long enough to drink. I hoped the small bucket I was using wasn't too deep. I had to balance it on the stiff, dehydrated remains of her foal to place it right under her lips. I stepped back to her shoulder and placed my hand on her back.

"It's up to you, babe," I whispered. "I'll help you all I can, but if you prefer to let go, that's okay too. But I'm gonna give you the choice."

I pulled the wad of hay from under my arm and laid it next to her feet. I didn't want it on top of the foal.

She lowered her head an inch farther until her lips touched the water. I smiled when I saw her swallow . . . and again. She slowly moved her head toward the hay without stepping back, as though afraid a step would unbalance her.

Clipboard man had loaded a light bay next to Hobbit.

"Who else did I get?"

He looked at his list. "Sugar in My Tea."

"Sugar it is."

He closed the back doors of the trailer as I used another bucket to refill the one in front of the gray mare, but she made no move toward it. I ignored the incredulous looks from the faces along the fence.

He had gone into the barn and returned with manila envelopes. "Look, lady, even if the horse has the strength to load, I'm sure it'll just be an expense to haul off her body."

"My name isn't Lady. It's Jillian," I said as I stuck out my hand. "Yours?"

He hesitated until I was starting to feel like an idiot, but he finally reached out a gloved hand to shake mine. "Gage."

"What's in the envelopes, Gage?"

"Instructions on how to feed malnourished horses, when to worm, and their medical histories," he answered, handing them to me.

"I'll be back in three-and-a-half to four hours, Gage. Or will you be gone by then? Will it be a wasted trip?"

"Well, the pickings will be a lot slimmer."

"That's okay. I'll take whatever is available. You'll probably be off duty by then."

"No, I usually stay until no one else is coming."

"Will you be able to get away for something to eat and a break?"

"There might be a lull, but I didn't think to bring a lunch."

"Here." I tossed him my brown bag of sandwich, carrots, and pretzels. I slammed the door shut and let the truck roll forward.

It was the hardest trip I've ever made. I wanted to hurry but forced myself to take it easy. I didn't want to traumatize the horses any more than necessary. I kept listening for a thud that would indicate one or the other had collapsed.

I breathed a sigh of relief as the farm came into sight. I couldn't help notice how nice the repaired part of the fence looked. Despite his young age, Joaquin had done a wonderful paint job. I decided that at some point, I'd have the whole fence repainted so it would look as good as the repaired part.

Sergio came down the apartment steps as I backed the trailer as close to the paddock as I could get. My back complained about sitting for so long as I slid from the cab. I held my breath as I opened the trailer doors. Both horses were still standing and turned their heads as if to ask "Are we there yet?"

I left the horses standing in the trailer to give them time to get their land legs back. Sergio had a stall bedded thickly with straw. "Great job, Sergio, but let's put them in the paddock for now. It's a warm day. Sun and open space will probably reassure them more than four walls and clean straw. We'll bring them in this evening. In fact, if I'm not back from this next trip by six this evening, go ahead and bring them in. That'll give you time to prepare three more stalls with bedding and a half flake of hay."

The paddock had been a sacrifice area for the previous owners' horses, and there were only a few clumps of grass here and there. I wouldn't have to worry about the horses gorging themselves. We put about a fourth of a flake of hay on the ground for each horse with a good bit of space between them. Sergio told his son to run water into the new water trough.

While it was filling, I gave the okay to unload the horses. Sergio calmly backed Hobbit out of the trailer slow step by slow step. As soon as she was clear, Joaquin walked quietly into Hobbit's side of the trailer, speaking quietly in Spanish to Sugar. As soon as she was aware of him, he touched her to let her know where he was at all times. He calmly ducked under the divider, untied the lead, and slowly and gently began to back her out, following his father's example. I so wanted to unload them myself, but I needed to know how Sergio and Joaquin would handle them in my absence.

I followed them into the bare paddock to give them some soft caresses before leaving again. I went to the house for something to eat and suddenly realized how tight my shoulders were. I tried to relax them. I wished I had time for a hot broth to wash down my sandwich, but it had taken a good while to unload the horses and I felt the need to get moving. I got back into the truck feeling exhausted and dreading the trip. I turned on the radio and made it loud. I wondered if they'd criticize me if I didn't show up for another two horses. But I had promised the gray I'd give her a chance. I had to finish what I'd started.

As I drove, I thought about Joaquin's confidence. It obviously came from Sergio. I had witnessed the hose in a tangle when Joaquin was trying to drag it to the trough. His father had showed him how to untangle it and then let the boy continue. No yelling or criticizing. I was even more determined to put something in the yard behind the garage the hardworking children could enjoy.

It was four o'clock by the time I pulled into the abandoned farm once again. Half a dozen mares still stood near the water trough or small piles of hay. The gray, however, stood where I'd last seen her. Gage tried to intercept me as I headed toward her. My heart was soaring. She had decided to live. She had a new stench about her. Liquid feces coated her hind legs as though the water I had given her had gone straight through her system.

"Take your pick," Gage called, trying to distract me.

"Any of them," I answered without looking his way.

She saw me coming and tried to raise her head. Was she greeting me? I was thrilled that my small act of giving her a bit of nourishment caused her to acknowledge me. Most of the hay was still there, but I could see she had nibbled at it. I knelt on one knee next to her head and placed a hand lightly on her shoulder. Despite the pain screaming in my knees, I quietly said, "Hello, girl. Are you ready to go home?"

She was able to bring her muzzle to my leg to slowly lip my pants, and then she heaved a sigh. It seemed to take the last of her strength. I saw her knees begin to shiver. They buckled, and then she dropped with a thud. Her bony shoulder had grazed me just enough to throw me onto my backside. I sat there stunned, and then the tears streamed silently down my face.

I could feel the wet muck of the paddock seeping through my pants and kept telling myself to get up, but my body wouldn't respond.

"Here."

I looked up at the voice and saw a blurry gloved hand reaching down for me. I took it, and he pulled me up. I expected him to say "I told you so," but he didn't. With a hand on my shoulder, he guided me to the truck. I was grateful the fence-sitters were no longer there.

"I have Ray loading Remember Me. Stay here. I'll see what else I can get for you."

I thought about the name as I got a towel from behind the truck seat to put under me for the trip home. I blew my nose and dabbed my eyes. I would never forget her. I poured a cup of sweetened black coffee from my thermos, leaned against the fence, and watched Gage slowly return and load a chestnut with a blaze and white socks on both her front legs. As thin as she was, I was surprised she could even walk. I looked around at the remaining four mares. They were indeed the worst conditioned of the herd.

"That's Running on Empty."

"We all do at times," I quipped. Not wanting to look him in the eye, I spoke to the paddock fence. "Sorry I wasn't of more help."

"We appreciate you taking so many of them. Will you be able to get a vet to them within a day or two?"

"Yes."

"Wait here. I'll be right back."

I got into the truck cab to wait. Gage came out of the building with the familiar manila envelopes, paused and then jogged over to where the gray lay, and got the small bucket I had used to water her, emptying it as he walked back to the truck. I watched him in my side-view mirror as he brought it and slid it quietly behind the seat while handing me the envelopes and saying, "These are the medical histories on these two. Someone will be over in a week or two to see how you're doing and uh . . . to be sure your place is okay to leave them there."

"That's fine." I wasn't offended by the distrust, and I was sure my place would meet their standards.

"You look exhausted. Going to be okay to drive home?"

"Yes."

"Don't be afraid to pull over for a rest and some coffee. You've had a long day."

I turned the ignition, and as the truck rumbled to life, I felt his gloved hand on my shoulder. "Thanks for the lunch. It gave me the energy boost I needed." He paused and then added, "You know, I think she held on just to thank you for your kindness."

A sob escaped my throat, and the tears flowed like a spring stream full of the force of snowmelt. I had to bow my head on the steering wheel as my shoulders heaved. After a while, Gage walked away, probably feeling impotent in the face of such uncontrolled emotion and sorry that he had turned on the faucet with his comment. It was only the thought of the horses in the trailer facing an hour-and-a-half trip that helped me get a grip. I blew my nose, wiped my face, poured the rest of the coffee from the thermos into my travel mug, and put the truck in gear. I was out on the road before I remembered I had brought clean clothes just in case. Too late now. I didn't want to pull over to change. I just wanted to get home.

CHAPTER FIVE

The nearest large-animal veterinarian was in Montaine, twenty miles to our east. Dr. Madison Kurt came the next day to give them a general exam and to show us how to calculate their weight. The ferrier came on the fourth day to start the job of trimming their hooves back to normal length. It would be a gradual process as everything else had to be gradual.

We took 2 percent of their body weight and divided it by four meals a day. Each meal consisted of a cup of senior feed with corn oil added, a handful of alfalfa hay, and the rest made up of grass hay. They had mineral blocks and plenty of available water. The nights were still chilly, so we brought them into their stalls for their last meal, and they got breakfast before they were taken back out to the paddock in the morning. On the way to their daytime enclosure, they were permitted a bite or two of grass.

So the mares wouldn't fight over the food and eat themselves sick, Sergio, Elena, and I each put a horse on a lead to keep them away from one another while they ate their outside meals. Joaquin brought out the rations on a wagon. Milagro opened and shut the gate. After putting the feed pans on the ground, Joaquin and Milagro came to take Remember Me's lead so I could move Hobbit away from her a bit. Then we stroked, brushed, and crooned to our charges as they munched their meals.

Remember Me had been rechristened Nanny as she seemed to take to the children. I had even seen her place herself between them and one of the other horses when the pushing and shoving for food had gotten rough. I wondered if it was my imagination, but her other actions around them made me think not. Whenever the kids went into the paddock, Nanny made her way toward them. Nanny had lost her own foal when her malnourishment caused it to abort. And still she had this need to protect the young. Was that something that crossed the species' divide? At first, I was concerned about Mila and Joaquin being in among the horses, but they were always quiet and moved slowly. None of the horses seemed to mind. I often saw Sergio watching them, so I felt that if he was comfortable with it, I wouldn't make a fuss. I renamed Running on Empty Fancy because of her blaze and white socks.

Now I had a reason for getting up when the proverbial rooster crowed. The horses gave structure to my days. I could no longer wander around saying I would exercise, paint, or write later. I knew I had to do things now because later would be a feeding with or without a grooming. Or the vet or the ferrier would be coming.

I usually met Sergio coming down the stairs. We said our "good mornings" with smiles and fed the ladies while discussing what I wanted done that day or what Sergio thought needed done.

The horses were usually a bit stiff from being confined to their stalls at night. I was looking forward to when it would be warm enough to leave them out all night. The daytime showers were warming and helped wash the caked mud and manure from their emaciated bodies. We all used soft brushes over their protruding bones to help gently work the grime loose.

Our lives revolved around the feeding schedule. No one needed reminding. Without a word, we were all walking toward the feed room to get the leads and rations. Fancy seemed to be the dominant mare. She quickly caught on to the feeding schedule and was usually at the gate to meet us. Sergio or Elena would snap on the lead shank and lead her away. The other horses moved out of her way. Sugar was next. I always led Nanny and Hobbit until the feed pans were down. Then I led Hobbit away from Nanny to her own senior feed.

Hobbit always kept her eyes on me. I was surprised the first time I noticed, but I always watched after that and noticed she never failed. When I started meeting her eyes with my own and adding a rub on her forehead, she added a nicker. She was definitely my horse. I began to hope she would recoup enough from her ordeal to be ridden. I couldn't believe she was a low horse in the pecking order of the herd. She was huge and, in full weight, would be built like an old-time locomotive engine. She could easily have ruled the pasture. *Was her nature just too gentle?* I wondered. *And what did she see in me that made her single me out to be hers?*

I had made everyone a pouch in which to carry treats, a brush, a hoof-pick, and a rolled lead so our hands could be free when we went to the horses. Whenever we went to feed, I'd slowly slide the soft brush over Hobbit's hide, which was slowly shedding out and trying hard to respond to the vitamins with a shine. I could hardly wait for these poor bags of bones to start looking like real horses. I gently scratched her withers. She turned her head to look at me with those liquid, trusting eyes; and I marveled that in such a short time of retiring and attaining my dream farm, it had expanded to include a boarding family and four head of broodmares.

I could hear everyone else talking to their particular horse as they petted, brushed, or despite the protruding bones, leaned lightly against the sun-warmed bodies. I smiled at the soft hum. I couldn't believe how weak my arms still were. I would brush a short while and then need to rest them before continuing. And then, as we knew it was time to feed, we knew it was time to leave. We exited the gate, the wagon rattling noisily behind Joaquin, and turned to watch as the horses searched for missed wisps of hay or stray blades of grass. We went back to the in-between-feeding activities, them chatting to one another in Spanish and me going to my empty house, feeling Wee Shee's eyes watching me.

We all watched for signs of increasing weight and strength as if we would see a difference from feeding to feeding. Every Sunday, Sergio and I calculated weight and refigured food rations. We carefully increased the time allotted for eating grass—a few bites . . . one minute . . . two minutes . . . three. Their rations increased by a handful . . . a cup . . . a partial pound, and we greedily watched for results.

By the end of May, the corn had been sown in the field, and we were all working at planting the vegetable garden. We all looked forward to the breaks to feed the horses. We chaffed at what appeared to be no progress, but Dr. Kurt warned of horses foundering on too much grass and eating themselves to death with access to unlimited amounts of food. So we worked on developing our patience. We looked closely at the depth of the crevices between the ribs and thought we visually measured flesh filling in the ruts.

It was going to be an early summer. The spring rains had been downpours but had become little more than showers by the end of May. The nights were now warm enough to leave the horses out twenty-four seven, so we no longer needed to clean stalls. I missed it despite the pain it caused in my back and knees. We watered the garden every other day. I bought a play set that was a combination of a tree house, swings, and a tunnel slide for the kids. Their squeal of delight made me feel better about the work they were expected to perform.

Elena started LPN classes the first week of June. We cut, dried, and baled the first cutting of hay that week also. Sergio and Joaquin were now painting the frontage fence. Milagro and I helped with hoeing the garden. Although neither one of us lasted very long at first, we gradually increased our endurance. I helped carry fifty-pound bags of feed and forty-pound bales of hay. And then I'd have a soak in a hot Epsom salt bath, the hot, soapy water and hand lotion unable to remove the calluses from the palms of my hand that were once so soft. I decided I had better get gloves.

Even though I was out among Sergio and his family helping with the work for as long as I could stand the pain, my strength gave out, or the job was done, I then went my way; and they would begin to chatter. It made me feel I was intruding and, therefore, very lonely.

Wee Shee began to bring a black concoction for me as I would finish what I could manage of each chore. It had a bitter taste, but she kept motioning for me to finish drinking it. I looked to

Sergio and Elena for assurance, but their attention and chatter were already to their children. I downed it in a gulp and grimaced. Wee Shee took the cup, turned, and left without another word or gesture. Once again feeling very lonely, I went to the house, determined to enjoy an isolated activity.

Later I went out to help feed then sat on the redwood swing and watched fluffy clouds float by, followed by light-gray ones and those tracked by dark thunderheads amassing on the horizon as though preparing for an assault. I was grateful for the coming rain, and the rumble of thunder didn't bother me. But the wind was kicking up, shaking the tree branches threateningly. I headed for the paddock. Sergio, Elena, and the kids were coming from their yard behind the garage. We saw lightning in the distance.

We were all at the gate with leads. Sergio took Fancy, who was dancing as swirling dirt struck her legs. Elena snapped a lead onto Nanny and handed it to Milagro with soft Spanish words. I hoped they were words of instructions to remain calm and go slow, but still my stomach lurched. Would the horse still be child friendly in this wind? I calmed somewhat as Elena snapped a lead to Sugar's halter and followed close to Nanny's head to help if necessary. Both horses danced a bit but didn't pull on the leads.

Hobbit let me snap on the lead and then raised her head, facing into the wind as though to defy it. Or maybe she was remembering what it felt like pounding around a racetrack with the air rushing into her face, a jockey pumping on her back and swinging his stick in time to her strides.

I was dwarfed next to her. "You miss it, big girl?"

Hobbit bobbed her head, gave a half buck, and danced the rest of the way to the barn. I took it as a good sign that even though bones still showed, they were feeling pretty good.

Joaquin had been filling water buckets. The first clap of thunder made us all jump. "I'll finish. Go ahead before it starts to rain," I called.

Elena and the kids didn't wait for confirmation. They scurried to the door and then broke into a run, Milagro squealing as the first drops of rain caught them in the open.

I hung the buckets of water as Sergio gave them their afternoon hay and grain. I got out the grooming tools and waved him away. "Go be with your family."

He smiled. "Gracias."

I gently brushed the horses and picked hooves that, having had several trimmings, now looked more like normal hooves. As the lightning flashed and the thunder followed, I braided Hobbit's forelock. The lights flickered and went out. As I waited, I listened to the mares rustle in their straw, take deep swallows of water, lick their salt blocks, and munch their senior feed.

Hobbit stood straining against her stall guard, watching the pouring rain at the end of the aisle. I stood there watching her, wondering what she was thinking, remembering, wishing.

The lights came back on. The rain slowed as the clouds emptied their burden and let the late-afternoon sun through once again. It looked like it was over. I took the horses back out to the paddock. I picked the stalls, swept the aisle, scrubbed and emptied the water buckets, and prepared the evening rations. Right on time, the others arrived for feeding.

"I think it'll be okay to leave them out. It feels nice. The sky is clear."

We all gave the horses a final pat on the neck and went back to our respective abodes. Wee Shee intercepted me with her black brew. I guess it was becoming a habit as I didn't question it. I simply chugged it down as fast as I could to get past the taste.

As evening turned to night, I headed for my hot soak as I usually did to ease the pain in my body. As I was running the water, however, I realized I wasn't hurting nearly as bad as usual. Was it a miracle? Was it because my mind had been engaged all day? Or was Wee Shee's offering a pain medicine?

The next day, to answer that question, I passed up the morning dose of the bitter liquid; and even though I did no heavy work, I was in severe pain by evening. When Wee Shee offered the drink the next morning, I didn't refuse.

CHAPTER SIX

It was the Fourth of July when Gage finally showed up. The kids were in their pool. The horses had had their second meal. I had spent the morning making some picnic menu items and was lying on a blanket with a book. My hand rested on my growling stomach, my mind registering that it was a bit flatter than what it used to be, when I heard the tires on the gravel. As I walked to the parking area, Sergio kept his attention on the grill where raw steaks hissed as he put them on to cook and hot dogs were waiting their turn.

I couldn't help but smile when I finally recognized him as he got out of his truck. I remembered that someone should have come to inspect my facilities.

"I'm sorry, Gage. Did I misunderstand? Was I to call someone to come inspect my place?"

"No. We've just been really busy. I don't usually make inspections, but our main inspector moved south to be with family. We don't usually inspect on holidays, but I didn't know when else I could work it in. We aren't very organized. Somehow we lost your phone number but still had your address . . . Well, we had *an* address. We hoped it was yours."

"Lucky you, it is. Are you inspecting more than mine today?"

We were walking toward the stables. "Nope. Just yours."

"We're having a bit of a holiday cookout. You're welcome to stay. If you've been busy over the past months, you probably could use some downtime."

He smiled.

"Oh shoot, I'm sorry. Maybe you have a family outing?"

"No. My parents are dead, and sis lives in California. The ex has the kids. I'll probably just go home to watch a movie or read a book."

"Well, if our conversation doesn't thrill you, I have both movies and books here. You can still stay for the meal."

"Sounds good. Thank you."

"Well, here are the stables. The horses are out most of the time unless it's excessively hot or storming. The paddock is pretty bare, but we're up to about an hour a day on grass. Dr. Kurt says by fall, we should be able to put them out on pasture twenty-four seven. They've greatly increased their food allowances." I chatted on as we walked around the stables to the paddock. "And here they are."

At the sound of my voice, the mares raised their heads from dozing. Fancy came to the gate, but the others stood where they were to wonder what was going on.

"Wow, they look good."

"That's what Dr. Kurt says too. We can't see it even though our weight calculations increase."

"That's because you see them every day."

"I know it's a bit early, but will they be rideable after they've fully recovered? Or don't they ever fully recover?"

"It depends if they had any injuries before they were retired as broodmares. Did you read the vet reports I gave you when you picked them up?"

"Yes. I don't remember reading anything about injuries."

"Then it should be fine to ride them. Now that gray you were headed for that the other woman wanted? She has navicular disease that will put a limit on riding her."

"My gosh, how do you remember such a detail from two months ago?"

"I've been in this business long enough to know which of the foster people are really there to help and which are just looking for cheap mounts for themselves."

I felt my face flush. "Maybe I'm guilty of that. I know this started out as a foster venture, but we've put so much time and effort into these ladies, somewhere along the line I forgot about the possibility of having to give them up."

Out of the corner of my eye, I saw him turn his head to look at me.

"How much does it cost to adopt?" I questioned.

"It depends on how much we've had to put into them, whether they'll be rideable, whether they'll have special-care issues."

"I see. So these horses will probably be high-priced adoptions?"

"Normally, yes, but I remember you kept saying 'Load whatever can make it to the trailer,' and 'Preferably what no one else wants.' So Lady Luck will smile on you. You're taking good care of them. They're doing great. If we deducted what you put into them, we'd owe you. So if you're serious about wanting them, we'll just delete them from the adoption list."

I smiled broadly. "Yes. I'm serious about wanting them."

"Will I need to take you off the foster list also then?"

"No. There are still plenty of empty stalls. But give me some time to get these in better shape, unless it's an emergency."

He snorted. "It's always an emergency, but I'll keep that in mind."

"I guess that means my place passes as a fostering facility?"

It was his turn to grin, crinkling the skin at the corners of his brown eyes. "It does."

"Well, come on then. I'll show you where the books, movies, and magazines are. You don't have to stay in any area. Feel free to wander around."

He picked up a *National Geographic* from an end table and then plopped himself down on the blanket where I was reading and promptly fell asleep. I let my book fall to my lap. I couldn't help but gaze at him lying there breathing softly. His body was lean from hard work, his skin tan from the outdoors, his face relaxed from contentment. I guessed his age to be mid to late thirties. I couldn't help but feel a longing that I had met such a man earlier in my life. I could feel my facial muscles drooping as I began wistfully wishing he were closer to my age. Then I realized how idiotic it had been to give him the run of the place. He could have cased the house for later or picked up anything that caught his fancy. I mentally whipped myself for being so naive and trusting. Not everyone involved with rescue work would be honest through and through. But I couldn't believe that of Gage. I felt a flame of hope that he was much older than his looks. How else could he have time for this work unless he was retired?

I picked my book back up, but my eyes traveled over and over the same lines without seeing the words. Maybe . . . just maybe . . . *Some men have fallen in love with older women*, I mused. A smile played about my lips, my eyes glided back to the recumbent Gage; and I was shocked back to reality by seeing Wee Shee standing on the other side of him, barefoot, in her pale plant-fiber dress, her black eyes staring at me.

The smile dropped from my face. I hastily got up and walked out to the redwood swing where I could daydream in private. I refused to look back at Gage or Wee Shee. That was not easy. I focused on feeling the sun on my face. I started to recite my blessings list. And then I saw Milagro running toward me. I assumed correctly that the meat was ready for eating. She skipped by my side, accompanying me into the house to carry out the other food. Gage met us as we were coming out, Milagro holding the door for me.

"Anything else?"

"Here, you can take this. I'll go back for more." He took the bowl of potato salad and the veggie tray. I went back for the fruit salad and a sheet cake decorated as a flag.

I had gotten steaks for the adults, thinking the kids would be satisfied with the hot dogs. Wee Shee was nowhere in sight. Elena and Sergio ate hot dogs as well, leaving the three remaining steaks to dry out in the cooling grill as my heart felt it was drying out with rejection inside my chest.

Gage asked questions about the farm and my plans for it. I shared my dream that it would eventually be self-sustaining, complimenting Sergio's hard work and knowledge. I surreptitiously glanced at Sergio, but he was tickling Milagro, who sat on his lap laughing and trying to wiggle away from his tickling fingers, her hot dog waving in the air and dripping ketchup. The small family had chosen to sit apart. Elena had brought a blanket, and they sat on that as if having their own picnic. I was embarrassed and hurt, but Gage chatted on, asking questions about me and the farm, watering the hope in my parched heart. I wanted to smile smugly at Wee Shee, but she had not appeared, so I kept my eyes on Gage's handsome face.

Our eating had concluded when my interior clock alarmed. I glanced at my watch, and simultaneously, we all rose from our places. Gage glanced around, surprised. I had to laugh.

"We're just all so tuned into the feeding schedule we respond at the same time."

"Okay if I follow along?"

"Sure."

We went through the routine in silence. Gage watched quietly. As we went back to the picnic area afterward, he said, "I don't think you need to use the leads anymore."

"I know, but I enjoy that time with Hobbit. I think the others enjoy it as well."

"I have the feeling the horses enjoy it too. Looks like you've got company," he added as he put the leftover steaks on a paper plate, picked up the grill brush, and started scraping on the charred bars.

"Gage, you don't have to do that."

"It's the least I can do for you sharing your day and meal with me."

"It was a pleasure. And that truck is our vet. Don't know why she's here though."

I should have walked to her truck to talk to her there. I didn't. Why didn't I? Did I want to show off this gorgeous man that had just spent an hour's sleep on my lawn? Big mistake.

After a smile and a wave directed at me, her eyes couldn't help but slide to that gorgeous man and couldn't slide away again. I felt my heart crack. I cleared my throat so the crack wouldn't reach my voice. I forced a smile to my lips. They were stiff and cold; it hurt.

"Dr. Kurt, this is Gage Steele. He's the adoption coordinator of Equine Angels." I turned to Gage, and the halves of my heart fell apart. His eyes were glued to hers. "Gage, this is our veterinarian, Dr. Madison Kurt.

Gage just nodded his head toward Madison as though he didn't trust his voice.

"What can I do for you, Dr. Kurt?"

"Oh, Jillian, I'm sorry." She grinned. "I was a bit distracted for a moment. And please, I've asked you to call me Madison. I was past here a couple weeks ago and saw you putting up hay. We've started another phase of the riding facility and have come up short on hay. Any chance you have extra you could sell?"

"Actually, I could sell you the whole of the first cutting."

"That would be great. When would be a good time to come get it?"

"Anytime. It's supposed to rain this Saturday, so I'd recommend before that."

"I'll see what kind of help I can round up and get started early tomorrow. I didn't bring my checkbook. We'll count bales and settle up tomorrow. Is that okay?"

"Yep."

"I can help," stated Gage.

"We'll probably be here by eight in the morning."

"That's no problem. I'll be here. I can follow you and help you unload then."

"You are a godsend. Thank you, Gage. And thank you, Jillian. See you in the morning."

The yellow truck was at the end of the drive before I trusted my voice to ask, "Is it a long drive home?"

"It is. I'd better get moving."

"And then a long drive back here in the morning. I have a spare bedroom as long as you don't expect me to keep you entertained." I guffawed. "That sounded risqué."

Gage grinned. "I knew what you meant. That's kind of you, Jillian."

"There's a television in the room. We'll be doing two more feedings. The bird-watching is great, if you're into that. There's an exercise room, the entertainment center has lots of DVDs, the computer room has plenty of books, there are leftovers for supper anytime you want, and the shower is right next to your room."

"Sounds good."

"All right then. Enjoy yourself. I'm going to clean up here. Thanks for scrubbing that grill."

"Let me help."

"After it cools off, the grill cover is just inside the garage, and the grill gets put back into the left corner."

We carried in the leftovers, and then we were all walking toward the horses for another feeding. Gage pulled the cart as everyone else grabbed their rations and leads. He stood on the other side of Hobbit, and as her huge body totally blocked us from each other's view, his voice came as out of the ether.

"You're an extremely kind person, Jillian. I'm privileged to know you."

The lump in my throat wouldn't let me respond. I swallowed several times, blinked, and blotted the tears away. When the others started to leave, I unsnapped Hobbit's lead and held it out, my arm extending under her chin. To his credit, Gage took it and left with the others. I stayed on the far side of Hobbit, kept the soft brush moving, scratched her withers, pinched along the crest of her neck, and knelt to brush her legs. When I stood back up, Hobbit turned to face me, put her velvety nose against my cheek, and stuck out her tongue, swiping it across my lips.

I barked a laugh. "Was that a kiss?"

She hung her big head over my shoulder. It felt like a hug. I needed that hug. I leaned into her and wrapped my arms around her neck. I felt her brace herself to support me, felt her protruding bones pushing back, and was ashamed. This horse that had been deprived of sustenance was supporting me—someone whose fantastic life's dream was unfolding faster than I had thought possible.

Quit the crying. Get on with life.

Because it was a holiday, I had been going to skip the exercise but now decided on a swim. I slipped in the back door, through the exercise room to the pool room. My suit was in the cupboard of the small changing room with the towels. I flicked on the switch to start the current. It was a challenge, as I was tired, to keep up with the flowing water. As I towel dried, I was thinking of a timer that would switch the current to a slower pace after so much time and a slower pace still after another set time. That way, I could still challenge myself and swim for a longer time after I began to tire and my strokes slowed.

My legs were still rubbery as I dressed. I thought of spending some time at my computer, but Gage was in there reading, so I softly went up the stairs to my room. I had a book at bedside I had read for a while. After the fourth feeding that Gage did not attend, I went to the kitchen for a yogurt. He was there eating one of the leftover steaks and a salad, his nose still in the book. He looked up as I came in.

"You have a great selection of interesting books, Jillian. I had a hard time picking one to read."

I smiled. "I'll take that as a compliment."

"You should. Could I borrow this to finish it? It would give me an excuse to come again to bring it back."

My heart leaped, and I shoved it back down with a reminder of whom he'd really be coming to see. "Sure. Just take good care of it. I'm real protective of my books."

"I will."

"Well, I'll leave you to your reading."

We sidestepped each other the rest of the day. He read, and I went to the paddock for the last feeding then sat on the swing watching the bats. When I came in, I heard the shower. When I heard his door click shut, I took my own and then crawled into bed to cry.

CHAPTER SEVEN

We had just finished the first feed when Madison showed up with a trailer pulled by a pickup with a flatbed full of workers. Gage was already in the hay barn working on adjusting a few bales to create steps in the layers of hay so the highest bales could be handed downward to those stacking them on the trailer. He had been right to assume there would be no loading conveyor.

Among the crew was a very slight teen girl. Even her brown hair was wispy. Her blue eyes were so light that they had an otherworldly look to them. The minute she was out of the truck, her attention locked on the horses. Madison came to my side.

"I brought Cindy especially to talk to your horses. Do you mind?"

Keeping my eyes on Cindy, who was walking toward the paddock, I questioned, "Talk to the horse?"

"Yes. She's an animal communicator. I thought you might like to know what they're thinking."

"Sure."

"Good. We'll just give her a little time with them."

I resisted the urge to go with her, but I kept a furtive eye her way. Nanny, Fancy, and Sugar all went to her. Hobbit looked her way but stayed where she was. My heart swelled with gratitude. So far, I was the only one she would approach on her own, and that made me feel special. That was something I had never felt, not even with Daniel. Of course, I acknowledged, it could be she was just honoring her low position on the herd's pecking order.

Cindy stood with her hand on their foreheads, her cheek next to their cheeks, or with forehead to forehead like she was doing a mind meld. And then she was walking toward Hobbit. Hobbit stood her ground. Cindy made no attempt to touch her in any way but stood looking up at her. I set my bale of hay down and watched. Hobbit looked at Cindy awhile and then raised her head and gazed in my direction, or so it appeared to me, before dropping her eyes back to Cindy. For a moment, they stood looking at each other. Then Cindy stepped forward to stroke Hobbit on her shoulder. Hobbit took a step back as though to step out from under the hand, but Cindy was already turning away, walking toward the gate, giving a stroke to each of the other horses as she passed.

I seemed rooted to the spot as Cindy came toward us. Madison jumped from the trailer and stood next to me as the teen neared.

"Jillian, this is Cindy Ley. Cindy, this is Jillian Debaum. What did her horses have to say?"

"They are the start of something special here, although Jillian doesn't know it yet. They're all so grateful to be here. The big black one, though, says she is yours alone, to give you strength for the work ahead. She is especially grateful for the kindness you showed her friend after everyone else had turned away. You have a great heart—"

"I knew that," interrupted Gage from behind me.

"—and when it feels drained, she will fill it again."

My eyes filled with tears casting rainbows on everything and everyone around me, including the big black horse in the paddock gazing at me.

I felt in a daze the rest of the day. I couldn't concentrate when I tried to read. When I worked on the exercise machines, my mind was thinking of Cindy and Hobbit. Why would my heart feel drained? What was going to happen to make me feel so?

The days of July became scorching, and rain became a faint memory. Sergio and the children were at work weeding the garden, occasionally mowing the yard, painting the outbuildings, mowing the pasture to keep in check the weeds that were the only things growing, checking the progress of the oats and corn in the fields, and keeping the cobwebs swept from the corners of the stables. By noon, they ate lunch and took siesta. By four o'clock, Sergio found more work to do, usually in the flower beds or orchard, bringing in whatever fruit had ripened. The children were free to play except for feeding the horses. Elena was home by five and made sure to come by with little Milagro to at least dust and vacuum.

One morning, I was barely awake when I heard a thud against the bedroom window that faced the backyard. I jumped from the bed in time to see the snowy owl still flapping her wings slide down past the sill and out of sight. I dressed quickly, stumbled down the stairs and out the back door, looking for the owl on the ground, sure that she was injured. The owl was nowhere to be found, although I did find a soft breast feather right below my bedroom window. I looked a while longer but could find nothing else of interest.

Just as I was ready to go back into the house, the sound of a vehicle refusing to start finally registered on my consciousness. I went through the house and out the front door. Sergio had the hood of their rusty old truck up. Elena should have left already.

"Elena, you're going to be late for class. Let me take you."

She looked at me in surprise. "Gracias."

"Let me get my keys."

As I got my keys and purse, I tucked the white feather in a book for safekeeping. Elena was standing at the car, waiting. As I walked her way, I called to Sergio, "Do you have any idea what's wrong with it, Sergio?"

"Carburetor, I think."

"Shall I pick one up for you at the auto parts store?"

"Si, gracias."

"I'm not a car person. What model, make, and year is it?"

I traveled as fast as I thought prudent, and Elena was only fifteen minutes late. I told her I'd pick her up at four thirty when the class was over. The auto parts store wasn't open yet, so I thought I'd have breakfast at the Clear Point Diner while I waited. I parked my car in the parking lot and headed for the door.

"Ms. Debaum."

I looked for the faintly familiar voice and saw Cindy being dragged by a stout rottweiler.

"Cindy, are you okay? I think your dog is a bit much for you to handle."

She laughed. "She isn't my dog. I walk her for Mrs. Coates. She doesn't always act this way. She's usually quite a lady, but when she saw you, she just took off. She's pretty sure she should belong to you."

"What would Mrs. Coates say about that?"

"She'd be pleased as punch as she wants to get rid of her."

"Why?"

"Duchess was Mr. Coates's breeding bitch. He died last month. Mrs. Coates wasn't involved in the business. I think she's afraid of Duchess because she's a rotty. But Duchess is a sweetie. She's housebroken, a bit rusty on her obedience training, however."

"I'm not sure how I'd be on training."

"I could come help a couple days until you get the hang of it." Then she added with a straight face, "And I could help with the horses."

"Ah, I see," I said with a smile. "Don't you help with Madison's horses?"

"I did when we lived in Montaine. But Daddy got a job in Drummond, so we moved here to Clear Point. The rents were too high in Drummond, so we found a place here. I really miss going to Phoenix stables."

"You didn't have your own horse?"

"No. We can't afford one . . . or a dog either."

"Well, Cindy, you can come help with my horses anytime you want."

Her eyes lit up. "Really?"

"Really."

"Can you take Duchess?"

I looked down at the big black dog leaning against my leg, staring up with pleading eyes. "Sure, why not?"

Cindy had a difficult time pulling Duchess away. We had arranged for me to drop by the Coates house after I got the carburetor. I had my breakfast, went to the pet store for dog bowls, dog food, shampoo, and a leash, and was at the parts store the second it opened. Cindy, Duchess, and Mrs. Coates were all sitting on the porch when I pulled up.

Duchess charged down the walkway and jumped up to greet me. "Augh," I scolded and turned my back to her. The jumping stopped, and when I turned back to look at her, she was sitting demurely with her head cocked.

"Good girl," I praised and was almost sure she smiled. "Heel," I commanded, and she fell into step beside me as I continued up the walk. "Mrs. Coates, I'm Jillian Debaum. Cindy said you wanted to get rid of Duchess."

"That surely would be a blessing. I just don't want to be bothered with the mess anymore."

"Does she have any special talents?"

"Having babies is what she does."

"Your husband didn't play ball with her?"

"He worked on obedience with her, took her to competitions even. I didn't think to keep all the ribbons and trophies. They were collecting dust, so I put them in the trash when Melvin died."

"Do you want something for her?"

She hesitated as though considering. "No. Just take her. You can have the rest of that bag of dog food as well. But I threw her pedigree papers away also, so breeding won't get you much."

"What's her registered name?"

"Duchess of . . ." She caught herself. "I don't remember the rest of it."

"That's okay. I appreciate the dog food."

"I'll get it," Cindy offered.

I gave Duchess a stay command and walked to the car to get the leash. When she saw Cindy carrying her dog food bag to the car, she broke her stay to dash to the car. I took her back to the original spot and gave the command again. She stayed but couldn't stop her body from wiggling all over and whining. I put the bag on the front seat, opened the back door, and called, "Duchess, come."

Like a locomotive, she charged down the walk and bounded into the car, her tongue lolling happily out the side of her mouth. I snapped the leash onto her collar ring before closing the door. I wanted some control when we got home as I wasn't sure how she'd react when she saw the horses. I rolled a window partially down to give her air but not enough for her to stick her head out. She sat quietly on the seat with her nose up close to the opening. I watched her in the rearview mirror and smiled. I had me a friend.

CHAPTER EIGHT

Duchess brought a whole new dimension to my farm. With her arrival, the rains started, the grass greened, and there was a slight cooling of the temperature and more muddy mess in the house for Elena and Milagro to clean up.

At first, Elena and Sergio were leery of her, and Duchess wasn't too sure of the children, but she stood still to suffer their hugs and kisses. I praised her through her ordeal.

On her first encounter with the horses, I put her on a "sit, stay" at the gate. Nanny, Sugar, and Fancy took one look at the big black whatever it was, whirled, and ran, kicking up their heels to the far side of the paddock. Hobbit, however, came to me as usual, and we walked together to the gate, where the two black animals touched noses. That was so like Hobbit to be the opposite of the other horses.

After Duchess proved reliable with her obedience, I allowed her to enter the paddock with me, giving her a heel command. I had to smile. She kept her body at my left leg but her eyes on the other three horses that trotted away. At least their fearful reactions were lessening, and I was thrilled that they felt good enough to kick up their heels or to trot away. Duchess would sit facing Hobbit while I brushed the huge black horse. Once, Fancy had gotten up the nerve to come investigate the dog; but before she could get close, Hobbit swung her hips her way and kicked out. Fancy stopped but didn't move away, and that was good enough for Hobbit. When Duchess and I left the paddock, Hobbit followed, still preventing Fancy from getting very close.

At feeding times, I put Duchess on a stay in the yard so there'd be no trouble, especially with Milagro and Joaquin in the vicinity. Another thing I was having fun with was seeing how softly I could give Duchess a command that she could hear and obey. And then I wondered how Cindy communicated with animals. So I tried thinking the commands. So far, it would get Duchess's attention, and she would look at me as if waiting for the command. I was determined to talk to Cindy about it.

One day after I dragged myself out of my flowing-current pool, Duchess, who had been watching from her spot on the sidelines, jumped in. I laughed and cheered, "Go, girl, go." As soon as I saw her tiring, I shut off the current, got her to turn, and used the stairs to get out. That became the routine each day. I thought it would help her lose some of the heft she had gained from inactivity after her previous owner had died. Walks with Cindy aside, Duchess was a big dog and needed much more than brisk walks to keep her muscles toned.

It gave me pause to wonder how I was going to accomplish that as well. I decided agility and maybe K-9 training would also help. So I picked up some books on agility training, started buying supplies to build the obstacles, and showed Sergio the plans and where I wanted the course to be. I also made an appointment with Montaine's veterinarian clinic to get Duchess spayed. There were four vets at Madison's clinic. Vickie Torrence and Connor Winston did only small animals. Doug Yost did both but was mostly sent out for the large animals, and Madison did both but also focused mostly on the large because the need was so great in the county. I hadn't needed the small-animal vets, but it was only coincidence that I hadn't met Dr. Yost yet.

The day I came home from dropping Duchess off for her surgery, there was an unfamiliar car parked in front of the garage. Cindy jumped from the waiting vehicle before I was out of my own.

"Jillian, this is my mom."

I extended a hand. "Mrs. Ley, nice to meet you. Cindy, I was wondering when you were going to show up."

"She's been nagging me for days now," confessed Mrs. Ley. "Truth be told, I'm working now also and then trying to keep up with the house—"

"I help. You don't have to do it all. That's just an excuse."

Mrs. Ley looked at her daughter. "I know you help, sweetie. You do a good job too, but I'm still tired and don't want to have to be running around all evening as well."

"I'm assuming we're talking about Cindy coming to help with the horses?" I didn't wait for an answer. "Where do you live?"

"The far side of town."

"Does she have a bike?"

"I don't think I want her riding alone that far."

"Okay, maybe Elena could bring her here after her class at the vocational school a couple nights a week and I could bring her home."

"That would be too great an imposition on you."

"Well, I can combine the trips with grocery shopping or trips to the feedstore. It wouldn't be a problem."

"Well, if you're sure."

"In fact, she could spend the night and ride back in with Elena in the morning sometimes." I saw the doubt in her eyes. "I know we've just met, but I do hope we become friends. And there could be all kinds of reasons Cindy would need a second place to stay, like giving you and your husband a night out without worrying about Cindy being at home alone."

"Oh, Mom, that would be so awesome. Pleeease?"

"Maybe once in a while. It depends on if you keep helping around the house."

"I'm going to get a bike too. I could ride in, ride back out with her, and then haul her bike back home. Wow. Sounds like a lot of possibilities, and we'd be getting so fit."

Mrs. Ley smiled. "Yes, it does."

"Can she stay now, or does she have chores? I could use her help."

She glanced at her watch. "I'm on my way to work now. I get off at four. If I passed this way to work, it would be more convenient, but I don't. Could you bring her home by five, or would that be too long?"

"Nope. We'll find something to do."

"But, Mom, I have my job too."

"Cindy, you can't have everything."

I interjected, "Do you need to go home then?"

"I walk Melissa Blose's dog every day at noon and Mrs. Powell's dog at two."

"Can you walk them together?"

"They don't get along."

"Well, we'll work around it. If you want to stay this morning, I'll make sure you get to Melissa's by noon. Do you have a key to get in your house after your job?"

"Yep."

"Okay then. Mrs. Ley, have a good day at work."

Mrs. Ley sighed, shook her head, rolled her eyes at Cindy, and got into her car.

"Okay, young lady, here's the plan. I want the horses on grass for two hours. Actually we only have time for one-and-a-half hours. I don't want to turn them loose in the pasture. I'm afraid we won't be able to catch them at the end of their allotted time. So we have to keep them on leads. Sorry you stayed?"

Cindy just grinned.

We got brushes and stuck hoof-picks in our pockets. We put Sugar and Fancy on leads first and took them to the pasture. Sergio had just mowed the previous week, so the growing shoots would be tender and tasty. We brushed the ribby horses and tried to pick hooves, but that part didn't go so well. The mares wanted to keep walking.

I closed my eyes and felt the summer sun on my face. The scent of horse and grass juice tickled my nose.

"Hey, where's Duchess?" exclaimed Cindy.

"I took her to get spayed this morning."

"I wanted to tell you her full name is Duchess of the Jingle Nation."

"Where in the world did he get such a ridiculous name?"

"He thought her pups would put lots of jingle in his pocket."

"Did they?"

"Yes. He sold them for a lot of money."

"Speaking of Duchess, I've been trying to give her commands telepathically. She looks at me but doesn't do the commands. May I ask how you talk to them?"

"I don't really talk to them. I just see them."

I was confused. "You see them?"

"I don't know how to explain it."

The horses didn't want to leave the pasture just as I feared, but it was time for a feeding. And when Sergio shook the grain bucket, we had a hard time keeping them at a walk back to the paddock. It wouldn't be long before the special meals would be a thing of the past.

Afterward we took Nanny and Hobbit to the pasture. They didn't want to leave after their allotted time either, but Sergio appeared as if by magic to shake a grain bucket, and the horses were soon back in the paddock with the others. Cindy and I went to the house for some lunch.

There was a blinking light on the answering machine. The message was from the Montaine veterinarian clinic asking me to return their call.

"Jillian, this is Dr. Torrence. I just wanted you to know Duchess came through surgery fine, but we did find cancer in the uterus. Hopefully, it hasn't metastasized. You can pick her up in the morning by ten o'clock."

"What happens if it has spread?" I asked worriedly.

"As it advances, she'll start to lose weight and energy. By the time she quits eating, she'll be in constant pain and will show it by being restless, unable to get comfortable or rest most of the time. Actually, I would hope you wouldn't let it progress that far before you take action."

"Will it progress fast?"

"We don't know that we have to worry about it yet. And even if it's elsewhere in her body, every case is different. So my advice to you is to treat her as the healthy dog she appears to be."

"Can't you do a CAT scan or something to see if it's elsewhere?"

"We could, but they're expensive. What would you do if it showed something? You'd just worry sooner than you need to. There is really no medical indication for one. I really think we got it all. I do commend you for taking the step to get her spayed. If you hadn't, I doubt she would have lasted a year."

"Thanks for calling, Dr. Torrence. I'll see you in the morning."

We didn't have much time before Cindy was to be walking Melissa's dog. I quickly sliced some summer sausage and some Colby-Jack cheese. I had Cindy wash some grapes while I grabbed a box of Wheat Thins and added small cans of blueberry juice to our supplies, and we had a picnic in the car on the way to town.

I was almost halfway home before I realized my face was stretched in a big smile. *I have another friend*, I mused, *even if she does like my horses better than she likes me.*

CHAPTER NINE

The summer was half over. The sun continued to suck the sweat from our bodies. My long hair hung heavy on my neck, and I decided it was time to cut it off. My life was too physical to accommodate it anymore. The continued heat made me long for an outside pool. It was good timing as they were now on sale. Installations had slowed also, so they could get it installed within the week. The carpenters I called to build a deck around it couldn't come for a month. That was only a minor glitch. We could still use it.

We brought in the second cutting of hay. It smelled sweet and healthy. We began putting the horses into the pasture overnight to let them enjoy the cool night breezes and warm rains. They had full flakes of hay every morning and afternoon now with about a quart of senior feed with the usual corn oil added. They were anticipating their night hours on pasture and were at the paddock gate as darkness settled in about nine thirty each evening. By six o'clock in the morning, they were at the pasture gate, willing to come in for their grain.

I still brushed the horses at the second hay feeding. The novelty had worn off for Joaquin and Milagro, so I excused them from helping. I even told Sergio he could skip coming as well if he had other things to do. Often it was time alone for me and the horses. I always did Hobbit last. If her hay was gone, she'd still stand enjoying our contact, whereas the others would walk away.

Occasionally, I made an extra trip to the paddock to visit the horses. The first time Hobbit trotted across the paddock to meet me with my brush, I rewarded her with an apple. The other horses heard the crunch as she chewed it, scented the sweet juice in the air; but by the time they got to us, it was gone. I had to laugh as Hobbit looked at them with innocent wide eyes, asking, "What?"

The agility course was set up behind the garage, beyond the children's play area that now also had a trampoline. Duchess seemed to enjoy learning to negotiate the obstacles. She was already losing weight from swimming, but I still wasn't having her jump very high or do much climbing. That would come as she got more fit.

Cindy was coming two or three times a week. Duchess, Milagro, and Joaquin were all glad to see her. She played ball with Duchess and then tag with the children. She'd bring ribbons, and we'd braid them into the horses' manes and tails. We started lunging the horses at the walk for about half an hour. Cindy hoisted Milagro aboard Nanny one evening and then set the horse to circling her. Milagro's giggles brought Joaquin to check out what he was missing. He stood shyly at the door. I called him over and gave him a leg up on Sugar. As she circled me, a huge grin spread on Joaquin's face. Cindy and I looked at each other and couldn't help the smiles that sprang to our faces as well.

Duchess lay inside the arena door, out of the sun, watching, wanting to be near but leery still of so many moving horse hooves. And then another form appeared in the doorway. Wee Shee stood watching the scene. I saw Duchess sit up and cock her head at the small terra-cotta woman just before Sugar passed between us. By the time the horse stepped out of my line of vision, Wee Shee was gone.

It was then that I realized that I had not had any of her bitter pain-killing brew in a week or so, although I sometimes still caught her watching me, always in her pale shift made of plant fibers. She no longer seemed out of the ordinary. I no longer felt intimidated by her stares. She was just part of our farm family. Sometimes I was even amused by her watchfulness. She would stand and rotate her head, surveying all. I smiled once, thinking how like an owl she was. Her piercing eyes looked straight at me, and one eye winked. The hairs on the nape of my neck stood at attention, and I lost my smile.

My clothes were fitting much looser. That encouraged me to buy the mountain bike I had been contemplating. I took to the road, pedaling only as fast as Duchess could trot. There were a few small hills or long grades. Without any instruction or urging from me, Duchess would lean into her collar to help me make it to the top.

She seemed always by my side, even as I soaked my weary body in a hot bath, and I found myself talking to her at odd moments and about odd things. I would be musing about the loneliness I had endured during my working life, my single-minded determination to attain my dream, and what powers had brought us all together to give me such joy now. And I was immensely happy.

One afternoon, a familiar truck pulling a horse trailer came slowly up my drive. *Probably returning the book*, I acknowledged to myself, *on his way to visit Madison*.

"Hello," I called as he put his pickup into park.

"Hello yourself. I brought your book back. I hadn't read for enjoyment in years. Thanks for getting me started again. Nice haircut."

"Thank you, and you're welcome. On your way to Phoenix?"

I saw a slight reddening at his temples, but he held eye contact. "Well, I was but not now."

"Why not?"

"Because of my load."

I started walking toward the rear of the trailer.

"I was supposed to transport this fella to a foster home over in Grant Station. I warned them the horse was in bad shape, but they assured me they'd take him. I wasn't even sure he'd survive the trip, but I kept hearing someone in my mind say they deserved a chance. When I got there and they saw him, they said they just couldn't do it."

I was opening the tailgate.

"Jillian, he might not even be alive by now."

But he was. He turned his hanging head just enough to be able to see the light I had let in. I wondered if he thought it was the light at the end of the tunnel.

"What's his name?"

"Sunshine. Sunny for short."

I looked for something beneath the mud and manure that would give a reason for that name and spotted a patch of dull gold. "Did you once bring sunshine into someone's life?" I asked him.

Milagro, Joaquin, Wee Shee, and Sergio appeared at my side. "Sergio, would you get a bucket of lukewarm water? I need a handful of hay also."

As I stepped up into the trailer, I heard Sergio speak rapidly in Spanish to the children, and they scattered to do his bidding. I kept my hand lightly on Sunny's hide. As I neared his head, he flattened his ears. "I'd be angry too, big boy. You have a right."

I heard Joaquin's running feet as he returned with the hay. I was just about to warn him to walk when he did exactly that before reaching the trailer. He carefully stepped up into the trailer and put his hand on the horse to let him know he was there.

"Be careful. He might bite," I warned.

Joaquin started talking softly in Spanish. When Sunny nipped at him, he pushed the hay forward so that was all the horse's teeth encountered.

"Good job, Joaquin," I congratulated through a smile. I mentally stored that trick in my mind for further use.

The water arrived, and we all got out of the trailer to give the horse a chance to refresh himself.

"I'll take him."

"Jillian, I doubt he'll survive."

"You knew that when you were taking him to the foster home. Well, here's a foster home, and I'll deal with whatever comes. What are you gonna do with him if I don't take him? Take him back to where you got him?"

Gage didn't answer. He just stood there looking at me.

"Look, unhook your trailer and go visit Madison. On your way home, stop by here. If we have him out of the trailer, you can hook up and be on your way. If he's still in there, I'll allow you to dispose of the body. If he simply needs more time, you can take my trailer if you think you'll need one."

Gage's mustache twitched, and the lines at the corners of his eyes creased ever so slightly. "It might be late."

"I'm not going anywhere. Why don't you pull the trailer around to the end of the stalls so he doesn't have to walk so far?"

"You might want to leave him out. It's hard getting a dead horse out of a stall."

"Was he abandoned in a stall?"

"No, a bare paddock."

"I want him to feel secure . . . Not like he's going back into the same situation.

Without another word, Gage slowly pulled the trailer close to the far door of the stall row. Sergio unhooked the trailer. Gage waved and drove away.

We had a contraption Sergio had built—four wheels, a bed of planks, and a pull tongue—that we used for transferring several bales of hay or straw at a time. I asked Sergio to get me seven bales of straw. He could have used the riding lawn mower to pull it, but Sergio must have thought the noise would bother Sunny. He was pulling on the tongue, and the children were pushing from behind.

"I didn't mean for you to do it the hard way, but thank you, Sergio."

We spread two bales loose for Sunny in the stall and then lined the other five bales side by side, the ends abutting an aisle wall. I went to the house for a blanket and a pillow. I put a few flakes of hay in the corridor for easy access during the night, a handful of grain in the feed pan, and fresh water in a clean bucket just inside the stall door. All that time, Duchess had been trailing me, watching with curiosity.

"It's okay, Duchess. We're just going to camp out in the barn tonight."

Sergio and the kids were called to dinner. I waved them away. I lowered the tailgate and went in with a handful of hay. "Are you ready to give this a try, big boy?"

His ears flattened, and his bared teeth swung my way. I had made sure my hand, full of hay, was on a level with his mouth. His teeth chomped on the green wad but nipped one of my fingers.

"Ouch. I guess having small fingers is a requirement of success, eh?" I crooned while he chewed, and I pulled at the slipknot. Then I slid in front of his chest and gently applied pressure. "Back up. Back . . . back . . . back . . ."

He took a step each time I encouraged.

"Good boy. Baaack."

I heard a hoof strike the metal ramp. We paused. I stroked his neck and down his shoulder but kept my left hand on his halter to prevent any sneak attack with his teeth.

"Ready? Let's take a couple more steps, okay? Baaack."

His front hooves hit the ramp as his back clomped on the aisle concrete. Feeling more secure, he took a few hurried steps to get completely down. But his back legs gave out, and he went down, leaning on his right haunch. His front legs shook, and I expected them to give way as well, but his knees remained locked, and at last, he stabilized in his sitting position, breathing heavily.

My mind was scrambling about what to do if he couldn't get back up when Sergio and Joaquin entered the stall row. They picked up speed without breaking into a run. Sergio asked no questions. He simply looked at me and waited.

"Joaquin, you come hold the lead and one hand on his halter. When we say, you pull forward and let him drop his head if he needs to. Sergio, help me rock him, and when he starts to get up, slip around to the other side so he doesn't topple all the way over."

Sergio and I got next to his hip and began to rock him. "Pull gently, Joaquin."

I could hear Joaquin encouraging softly in his melodic language. Sunny heaved his body. I slid lower to get more under his hip to support him. As soon as Sergio saw Sunny move his right leg under his body, he scurried to the other side. Sunny stood with his back legs splayed, body trembling, his head hanging, his breathing labored.

"I guess I shouldn't have moved him," I said apologetically.

"I think seeing a stall with clean bedding and food will give him more hope than to remain inside a trailer wondering what will happen next."

"I think you're right." I wanted to smile at him as I agreed, but my mind was wondering if he and his family had often felt the uncertainty of "What next?" during their journey into America. Had they experienced how hard it was to find bits of hope to keep them moving forward?

When Sunny's breathing slowed, we gave him a handful of senior feed and another drink. I heard some gurgling from his insides. He tried to lift his tail but didn't get it very far. The smelly brown liquid clung to the coarse long tail hair as it streamed down his legs. I went to the wash bay and got two buckets of warm water. I added soap to one and got a washcloth. I gently washed the horse's anus, back legs, and tail and then rinsed them. He had a few bloody scrapes where his haunch had hit the cement. I went for another bucket of clean, soapy water, clean cloth, and spray saline to doctor them.

"I'll bet he'd feel better if we could clean his whole body."

"I don't think he could stay up with all the rubbing," replied Sergio.

"I don't think so either. So which will be worse: trying to turn him toward the stall door or back him some more?"

"I think his legs will give out if we ask him to turn."

"You could be right."

I sloshed water over the feces on the cement to dilute it.

"Joaquin, ask him to back a step."

A step at a time was all he could do. We would let him rest and let him take another bite of hay, but the chewing seemed to tire him, and he lost interest in the proffered food. When we at last had him facing the door, all eyes went to the four-inch drop from the aisle to the matted stall floor.

"Do you want me to lead him in, Joaquin?"

The boy shook his head and began speaking softly to the horse. Sunny swiveled his ears, listening. Joaquin stepped into the stall. Sunny took the downward step and paused to brace himself before taking another. I saw him drop his nose to the clean bedding, inhale deeply, and let out a long sigh. He was still aimed away from his food, but we left him to turn when he wanted and went out to brush the mares and transfer them to the pasture.

Later I checked on Sunny. He still stood as we left him. Duchess and I went to the house for our supper. It was late, but I knew I wouldn't be able to sleep, so I grabbed a book and read until my eyes were burning. We headed for the barn. I crawled between the light blankets, my back against the wall and Duchess against my belly.

I awoke briefly when Gage hooked up his trailer and left. I awoke again, hearing Sunny shuffling toward his hay and munching softly. It was the smell that woke me the next time. I got up to get him another small pile of hay but saw that he hadn't eaten all the original ration. I tried to put the smell out of my mind. The sky was just lightening when I awoke again. The hay was still there, but I got him some senior feed. His breathing seemed labored. I was afraid to leave him, but I needed a break.

We went through our routine of feeding and grooming the mares. Then I got a soft brush to try to work the mud from his coat, but the dust I created seemed to make his breathing more difficult. I was starting to get upset. I didn't know what to do. Should I leave him alone, stay with him, or just visit often? Would his breathing be easier if he was outside? As I stood stroking his forehead, I heard footsteps.

"Jillian?"

"Madison?"

"Yes. Gage told me you have another abuse case."

I bristled. Sunny wasn't a case. He was a life.

"How's he doing?"

"His breathing is more labored."

She put her medical case down and removed a stethoscope to listen to his heart, lungs, and gut sounds. "More labored than what?" She lifted his lips and pressed on his gums, noting the capillary-refill time, and gave his teeth a cursory check.

"More than yesterday after any effort to move, I guess. I thought putting him in here originally would make him feel more secure. But now I think it was a mistake. Too much dust. I shouldn't have tried to groom him. He didn't eat more than a couple handfuls of hay while we were unloading him and last night. The senior feed I gave him is still in the pan."

"I think it would be a good idea to get him outside in the open air."

"I just wanted him to feel secure."

"I know. I brought some portable pipe fencing. This end of the stall row gets the afternoon shade. We'll just set up a small enclosure to the right of the door."

"What about the grass?"

"The enclosure won't be big enough for it to be a deciding factor, and if he isn't eating, it's probably a moot point. Just be sure to keep hay, the senior feed, and water available."

"It took us a long time to get him in here."

"But he was tired from the trip. He's had a night of rest and some food. I'll bet it goes easier. Here comes Sergio. We'll get the fence panels."

I snapped on his lead. "Shall we go outside, Sunny?"

He followed me willingly, and it did go smoother than the night before. It wasn't long before the enclosure was assembled around him. He had fresh water and fresh food.

"Jillian, I have to be honest, I don't expect him to live. At best, you'll be making his last days or hours more comfortable."

"If that's all I can do, I'll do it."

"If at some point you want to end his suffering . . ."

"Is he suffering much?"

"He's probably feeling better right now than he has in a long time. He's not an old horse, but look what neglect had done to him."

I couldn't help the tears that filled my eyes. I felt her hand on my shoulder.

"I think you'll know when it's time. Or if he gains more strength, we'll give him the benefit of the doubt, worm him, and draw blood to see what else we're dealing with. But right now, those things would be too traumatic. So I'll leave it up to you. I have a backhoe, so if you need a hole dug, let me know."

My head snapped to face her with a scowl at her suggestion, but she held my eyes, demanding I face reality. And eventually, I dropped my eyes and whispered, "Thank you."

Sergio was building roofed, three-sided windbreaks in the pasture and paddock. I told him I'd do Sunny's hourly feeding. I made sure I still groomed the mares and forgot about lunch. Duchess trotted after me back and forth between the horses.

Now that Sunny was in the open air, I again tried to loosen the filth attached to him. It was intermittent work, a little each time I went to check on him. So it took all day, but the job was finally complete. He was still dirty, but the clumps were gone. I had gotten his stall cleaned and spent another night in the barn. I brought an alarm clock to wake me every couple hours to see if Sunny was eating and needed another ration of food. When he had eaten, I was hopeful. When he hadn't, I was dismayed.

The next day, Sunny's breathing seemed easier, and his head was held a little higher. I washed his backside again, ministered to his scrapes, and brushed him gently over his protruding skeleton. I slept in my own bed that night after giving him a half flake of hay. Duchess and I both slept all night, exhausted from our vigil. We were greeted by a soft nicker when we took Sunny his breakfast the next morning. My heart jumped for joy but crashed immediately after seeing his previous night's food untouched. Still, his nicker gave me hope.

"Are you going to prove them wrong, pretty fella?" I scratched behind his ears.

After the sun passed its zenith and a cooling shadow appeared along the wall, I thought I'd spend time with Sunny just by being near him. I made myself comfortable with a book after giving Sunny some fresh food. I leaned against the wood that was still warm from the morning sun. Duchess stretched out beside me with her big head on my thigh. I stroked her silky ears and looked across the field to the road fronting my farm. I looked up at birds swooping through the air above us and wondered if they were getting ready for migration or just playing now that the chore of raising their young was done.

A moment later, Sunny took tentative steps toward me. I looked up and smiled at him. "Come on, big boy. You can do it."

I crossed my legs into an Indian sit so he could take a step closer. His nose came to my face as he exhaled. I saw his knees begin to shake. Duchess jumped up and barked. I had a flashback of a gray horse dropping beside me. I heard Sunny give out a long groan as his body slowly gave way to gravity. It was such a gradual collapse it looked as though he was resisting with all he had left in him. His head now lay in my lap. I saw my reflection in his dark eye. He slowly blinked twice, and I disappeared from view. He gave a last heavy sigh that sounded so much like contentment as his spirit slipped away.

I was stunned, unable to move, tears streaming down my face, feeling Duchess's tongue licking them away.

CHAPTER TEN

I spent the rest of that day alone. I swam in my flowing-current pool, letting my tears flow away with the moving water. I wrote in my journal, telling myself I had done all I could for Sunny. He had come to me, exchanged breaths with me, and let me know he appreciated my effort. I, Jillian Debaum, had brought comfort and peace to a suffering animal. I might have retired, but I now had another vocation.

I heard someone knock. I ignored it. I didn't want to be bothered right then. Duchess sat up and looked askance. I mumbled no. I heard Madison open the door and call my name. Duchess immediately thundered down the stairs, barking and snarling as she went. I heard the door slam as Madison quickly retreated. I smiled. That was the first time anyone had protected me. When Duchess returned with her tongue lolling out the side of her mouth, I held her big block head between my hands, laid my forehead on hers, and told her she was a good girl. She plopped her big body to the floor near my feet and lay panting from her charge.

I was up early the next morning to engage in our routine. Sergio helped bring in the horses. He assured me he had taken care of everything the day before. I thanked him and said I knew I could count on him.

"Would you like a day off? You've been working hard on those windbreaks. You could use some time-out. Take the kids and Wee Shee to the Disney movie playing at the theater."

"They would like that." He smiled. "But Elena has the truck."

"Take mine, and afterwards, stop by the do-it-yourself store and pick up a patio block. I want to use it as a headstone for Sunny."

"Why don't we make one? I'll pick up some cement. We have two-by-fours to block it in, and we can put on it nice writing."

"That sounds better, Sergio. Great idea."

I didn't do much besides brush the mares, standing for some time with Hobbit's head draped over my shoulder, my arms around her neck. I finally went to face Sunny's grave. I was so thankful that Sergio had taken the initiative to get the hole dug and to bury Sunny while I was withdrawn. I wanted to remember the big gold horse associated with that contented sigh and my reflection in his eye. As I felt my eyes filling with tears again, I said out loud, "Not gone. Just waiting on the other side."

I walked back to the garage for a shovel and dug a sixteen-inch-wide, twenty-four-inch-long, four-inch-deep depression at the end of the mound of earth covering Sunny's body. I wanted the frame to fit down in the ground so the top of the marker would be flush with the ground. While working, my mind thought over the difficult time we had getting Sunny in and out of the stall. I wondered if maybe we could put a door in each of the last two stalls leading to paddocks on the outside. The stalls could then be used as quarantine for new arrivals.

I got a pillow, my journal, and a book and headed for the redwood swing. I stopped midstride when I saw the snowy owl perched on the top of the frame. Duchess spotted it also and sat to cock her head just as she had at Wee Shee several days earlier. I started to redirect my steps to a different seat, but the snowy took flight across the yard to the chain-link fence. I watched fascinated as the owl glided in for a landing, then I continued to the swing. It wasn't until I was seated that I realized Duchess had continued toward the white bird with dusky patches. The huge owl was watching Duchess, who dropped to her belly and was still. When the bird looked away, the dog crawled a step or two closer and then froze when the bird looked back at her. I enjoyed the show that looked like play. I knew both animals were totally aware of the other's presence and actions. When Duchess was but five feet from the owl, they sat looking at each other for several seconds, and then the owl took flight and disappeared around the far side of the hay barn.

When Sergio pulled in ten minutes later, Wee Shee was there to greet them. I had to wonder where she had been all that time. Did she hide because she was afraid of me or of Duchess? I couldn't believe those dark, flashing eyes would back down from anything.

Elena arrived home at five o'clock, with Cindy hitching a ride. As they got out of the truck, I called to her, "Elena, today is a day off. I'm grilling chicken later. You're all invited."

She smiled and nodded.

Cindy and I went straight to the horses. We groomed and exercised them. Milagro and Joaquin both rode Nanny and Sugar again. Then I asked, "Do you think Fancy could handle you riding?"

"Not yet. She does feel left out, however, because she doesn't get to carry someone."

"Remind her that Hobbit doesn't either. Why don't you take her as your special project?"

Cindy's eyes lit up. "For real?"

"For real. Take care of her first, exercise her first, give her a kiss and a treat before you leave. When she feels strong enough, you'll be the only one to ride her unless you give someone else permission."

"It'll be just like she's mine."

"Yep."

Madison called that evening. "Just checking on you," she said cheerily.

"I'm fine. I just wanted to be alone, and Duchess was being protective. She's never acted that way before."

"That'll teach me to enter someone's house uninvited." She laughed.

"I do appreciate your concern. Would you come to dinner sometime so Duchess sees that you are welcome here?"

"I'd love to."

"How about next Sunday? And bring the whole staff from your clinic," I suggested.

"Sounds great. Are we permitted to bring spouses and friends?"

I felt my heart constrict, remembering who her "friend" was. "Of course. You can even bring more rescues."

"Jillian, maybe you should wait awhile. You really take it hard when they don't make it."

"I'm fine, Madison. I feel honored to make their last days or hours safe and clean. Maybe it'll give some of them hope to survive, and if not, that's okay too. I have Duchess and Hobbit to bolster me up."

"Okay. But if it gets to be too much of an emotional strain, you are permitted to say 'No,' 'Not right now,' or 'Give me a break.' Promise me?"

"I promise."

—

On Sunday, my phone rang at seven o'clock. I had just gotten in from feeding and putting the horses back to pasture. It was Cindy speaking very softly.

"Jillian, I was wondering if I could spend the day with you. Mom and Dad are going to visit some old aunts and uncles of theirs. There aren't any kids there. I'll be so bored if I have to go."

"Sure. I'm getting a lot of adult company for lunch today, but they might be friends of yours, so you can help serve or go spend time with Fancy."

"That'll be awesome. Let me ask Mom."

I could tell she put her hand over the transmitter as her yell was muffled. "Mom, Jillian wants to know if I can spend the day at her place. Can I?"

I had to smile at her subterfuge.

"Okay. I'm allowed. We go right past your place, so they'll drop me off."

I could hear the smile in her voice. "Do you know what time you'll get here?"

"They're leaving about eight, so probably by eight thirty."

"Then I'll see you when you get here."

No sooner had I hung up the receiver than the phone rang again.

"Jillian, this is Gage."

I laughed. "I was joking when I told Madison you could bring more rescues to the cookout."

"Oh."

I heard the disappointment in his voice. "I'm sorry. Do you really have another rescue?"

"It's pretty much an emergency. It's a pony that has been out on pasture twenty-four seven, which isn't bad, but the kids have randomly but often shot it with BBs. They hide, so the pony can't see where it's coming from. It's a nervous wreck, worrying when the pain is going to hit next. It's too distraught to eat and has worn itself down with pacing and running when it gets hit."

"Poor thing. By all means, bring it."

"Jillian, I was so sure you'd help. I'm almost to your place already."

"Then I'd better hurry to get a stall ready. I'm thinking he'll feel safer inside for a while."

Dr. Yost was on call that day and arrived shortly after we had the little slate-gray gelding in the stall. Gage explained that he gave the doctor a heads-up. The pony had large clumps of hair missing, which Dr. Yost thought was mostly from anxiety. He was really concerned at the level of agitation the pony had and was worried about him having a heart attack. He had just suggested a tranquilizer when Cindy arrived.

She came straight into the stall, tears welling in her eyes. She took hold of the cheek straps of the halter on either side of the pony's head and knelt down to be able to look directly into its frantic dark eyes. The pony took a step forward to put its head against her chest. Within the folds of her arms, it closed his eyes with a sigh and seemed to instantly fall asleep.

"Good girl, Cindy," whispered Dr. Yost. "I was really scared for him. You got here just in time."

I looked incredulously from Cindy to Dr. Yost, wondering what I had missed.

"I'll stay with him awhile," Cindy whispered back. Then looking at me, she asked, "Is that okay, Jillian?"

"Of course."

Dr. Yost took a syringe of paste from his bag. "If he wakes up, Cindy, give this to him just like you give a wormer. Okay?"

"Okay."

Dr. Yost, Gage, and I left the stall row. "What just happened?"

Gray eyes twinkled in a creased, tanned face. "I can't believe you haven't heard of Cindy's animal communication abilities."

"Yes, I have, but she just walked in and . . ."

"She was probably picking up his distress even as she came into the barn. Sure, he was away from that pasture, but he was in a totally new situation that added to his stress level. He was exhausted. Once she assured him he was safe—"

"She did that without saying anything?"

"Well, not out loud."

"Do you understand how she communicates with them?"

"Pictures maybe? I'm not real sure. Sometimes it seems there has to be more than pictures."

"Excuse me?"

"It's thought that animals think more in pictures than with words."

"So if I picture Duchess doing what I want, she'll do it?"

He smiled. "I suppose she would if she wanted to."

Gage interjected, "I gotta go, Jillian. Thanks for taking the pip-squeak. I'll see you in a few hours."

I waved as I continued my thoughts to Dr. Yost. "And once the pony felt he was safe . . ."

"He just gave in to his exhaustion and fell asleep. Don't rush putting him out to pasture. Cindy can really help with letting you know when he's feeling brave enough to go out."

"I thought I'd bring the mares in tonight. I'll put one on either side and across the aisle. Kind of like a protective shield."

"That might help."

"Will you be able to come for the cookout?"

"As long as I don't get called out. I am on call."

"Bring your wife. If you have to leave, I'll take her home."

"Thanks, Jillian, but I'm not married."

"Oh."

"Am I still invited?" He grinned.

"Of course." I smiled sheepishly. "Ever been married?"

"No. Just always too busy. College, vet school, working long hours at my own office. Having joined Madison's staff, I'm just now at a point where I'd be able to properly accommodate a wife, but I haven't met anyone that's tugged at my heart."

"Delayed gratification. Not many people can pull that off. Do you regret it?"

"I don't think so. It's been rough at times, but I remind myself it probably would have been rougher in a different way if I had married."

"Was there someone you were interested in?"

"Yes, but she didn't want to wait. I guess I can't blame her. She wanted a family."

His cell phone rang. I quickly said, "Duty calls. Hope you can make it back at one o'clock."

CHAPTER ELEVEN

Gage had inadvertently named the small pony when he called him pip-squeak. We called him Pip from then on. The mares were all interested in him. It didn't take him long to whinny his loneliness when we took the others out to pasture and he was left inside. We all spent time grooming Pip. I even led him to the open door of the stable row so he could see the other horses in the pasture.

One morning, we put the mares in the paddock. I had Sergio lead Nanny out last, and I led Pip right behind her. But when he got to the end of the stall row, he didn't have the courage to follow her out even though she called to him. He whinnied his distress in answer. He skittered from side to side, circled, and even reared, his coarse cream-colored mane and forelock dancing like sloshed milk. Still, he couldn't get himself to cross that invisible line. We gave up and put the mares into the pasture for the day.

Each morning, we gave him the opportunity. Each day he spent calling to the mares from inside his stall. Finally, I called the clinic. The receptionist, Mattie, answered.

"This is Jillian Debaum. I was wondering if we could use a mild tranquilizer on Pip to help him go outside. He really wants to. He just can't get up the nerve."

"I'll call Madison and get back to you."

"Thanks, Mattie."

The phone still hadn't rung an hour later when I heard a vehicle drive across the parking area gravel. I didn't recognize the pickup that parked close to the stalls. It looked like Doug Yost, but it wasn't the clinic's service truck. He waved and waited as I crossed to him.

"Madison is tied up at another farm. They asked me to come out."

"It isn't an emergency. It was just an idea. I hope this isn't your day off."

"It is, but we all liked the idea."

Sergio materialized beside us.

"Sergio, why don't you bring in one of the mares?" suggested Doug. "I'll give him a tranquilizer paste, and then we'll see if he can follow her back out."

I thought Nanny would be the best choice, but I said nothing.

"Normally I'd give a shot. They act faster, and most horses don't mind them. I'm sure it wouldn't hurt as much as being shot with a BB, but I don't want to remind him or make him think this is not a safe place," Doug said as he squirted the tranquilizer paste into Pip's mouth.

"I can understand that," I said.

I heard Nanny whinny. Sergio had picked her. Pip responded. We stepped back to let horse and pony nuzzle until Pip calmed slightly. While we waited, Doug held Nanny's lead while Sergio and I moved the other mares to the paddock and brought Sugar in to help.

"Let's give it a try," urged Doug.

With Sergio and me leading a mare on either side, Doug led Pip between them. We turned the mares loose but spent some time petting Pip. He danced and pulled at his lead. As soon as we turned him loose, he scurried to Nanny's side. The other three mares came to encircle him with their big bodies. His back barely reached their bellies, and he was clearly visible. We could see the little pony's legs shaking. Nanny nuzzled him, and Sugar used her teeth to scratch his withers until Pip calmed.

Sergio brought hay and placed some at the head of each horse so they could maintain their protective circle around Pip. He even managed to get some to Pip inside the circle although Pip wasn't calm enough to eat.

"Well, that's a first step," declared Doug. "What time do you usually take them out in the mornings?"

"About seven."

"I'll be here to give him another dose."

"If it's the paste form, I could give it. You shouldn't have to make another trip."

"That's okay. I'll want to check his progress. Don't be surprised if he's too tired to eat tonight. That's amazing the way the mares are protecting him. I've never seen that before, especially Thoroughbreds."

"Maybe because they all know abuse?"

"Could be. I'll bet it won't take too many doses before he can come out on his own. See you in the morning."

"Thanks, Doug."

"No problem."

Doug was as good as his word, showing up the next morning before seven to administer the tranquilizer. The horses spent another day in the paddock surrounding the little gray pony. By the end of the week, he was able to walk to and from the paddock without needing the medical crutch or using the mares as shields. He loved being groomed. He was eating well. We put him on vitamins immediately to help his hair grow back in. Pip even made friends with Duchess, who was almost as big as he was.

I had watched amazed one day as Duchess walked nonchalantly into the paddock and sat a short distance from the cluster of equines. Nanny stretched her nose out to touch Duchess's nose. Then Pip took a couple tentative steps, emerging from the group. Duchess backed away, and Pip took a few more steps. The dog lowered her front half in a play bow, wagging her docked tail furiously, then turned and ran, watching over her shoulder. Pip charged forward a short distance before wheeling and dashing back to the safety of the mares.

Duchess calmly walked back and sat again. Pip ventured forth again. Duchess touched muzzles with the pony and then backed away. When Pip followed, she play bowed, turned, and ran. Pip followed, circling the paddock. The mares lifted their heads from their hay and watched as if encouraging their child to take his first steps.

As they neared the mares, Pip jumped in among them again. Duchess patiently started the process again. When Pip tired, he folded his legs and lay near the mares. When his head bobbed in sleep, Duchess trotted back to the house, picked up my scent, and followed it to me sitting on a bench in the shade.

I leaned forward to take her big head in my hands to give it a rough shake. She gave me a lick with her big pink tongue. "Duchess, you are so special. I'm glad you chose me."

Pip made huge progress after that. He didn't need the mares as shields, not even on the first day we put them in the pasture. Duchess went along to play and distract Pip from any fear associated with being back in a big field.

Our days calmed and settled into routine again. When Cindy came, she took care of Fancy first and then helped with the others as well. I could tell Fancy was enjoying the extra attention and was really bonding with Cindy.

The pool was installed, and a cooling swim was added to our usual activities on the simmering summer days. But there was a golden glow in the atmosphere, as if warning that summer was nearing its end. Sergio and I were working hard to get the windbreaks painted. The frontage fence had been painted and looked good. My arms were stronger, enabling me to groom the mares longer. I heard the squeals of Milagro and Joaquin in their backyard playing with new passion in their own pool, on the trampoline, and in the jungle gym. It was as if we all had to play and work hard in the waning days before the cold weather would put limits on our activities.

Still, the first morning of school was a shock. Although the children always seemed to know what I said to them, they had never said anything directly to me, and I had never heard them speak English. So that morning, as I watched them walk down the lane dressed in their best, backpacks slung over their shoulders, I couldn't help but worry how they would do. Milagro would spend only half a day in preschool.

Duchess whined at the door. I let her out, and she fell into step with Joaquin and Milagro. She kept them company until they clambered onto the long yellow bus and then trotted back to the house. I sat with a cup of hot tea, finding it hard that school was starting so soon. There were still three weeks of summer left. I realized I'd probably see less of Cindy also, and suddenly I felt lonely. To combat it, I went down to the horses and groomed Hobbit. She put her big head over my shoulder in a hug. I heard a voice say "Let's go for a ride."

I stopped stroking the warm black neck and stepped back to look Hobbit in the eyes. "Was that you?"

Doubt rolled into my mind. That wasn't a picture. I was sure I heard the words. I stood stroking her forehead, thinking maybe I had just thought my wish. Still, what would it hurt to try? If she threw me, it was a long way down. I didn't want to break a hip and lie there till Sergio came to take the horses in for feeding. Besides, how would I get on? I turned and started to walk away. I could hear her hoofbeats following me. When we got to the gate, I pushed her over alongside it. Then I squeezed between her and the pipe rails and pulled myself up to the third one, having to bend my body in half to grasp the fourth top rail. When I half turned, trying to keep my balance, it looked like a long way to her body although she hadn't moved.

It's gonna hurt if I fall, I thought. But I raised my leg and slid it over her back. It was a stretch. Only my calf was actually across her back.

I'd have to give a jump sideways. What if I hurt her? What if she bolts?

She was aimed into the corner, so if she jumped, it would be sideways. My legs were starting to hurt in their unnatural position. I needed to take action. I pushed off the pipe gate. It rattled in protest, and Hobbit startled but held her ground. I had grabbed a handful of mane and clamped my legs tight about her body.

It took a moment for both of us to calm. Her vertebrae jarred against my tailbone, and her ribs, though not prominent anymore, were easily felt by my legs. I geared up my courage, put weight on my left hip, and gave her a gentle nudge with my heels. She turned out of the corner and walked along the fence line. I couldn't help but smile.

I let my pelvis rock with her movements and let my shoulders and legs relax. As we neared a corner, I touched her left side with my left heel and looked in the direction along the adjoining fence line. She turned out of the corner smoothly. I didn't think she had any formal training other than to break from a gate and run pell-mell down a track, but if my mental pictures and shifting weight gave her a hint that what she was doing was what I wanted her to do, it was a good way to start her schooling.

We walked along the total fence, and then she turned into the field and began to graze. I sat astride for a few more minutes and then slid clumsily and dropped heavily from her tall back.

"Thank you, Hobbit." I patted her neck, scratched behind her ears, and then walked back to the house. I had to record my first ride in my journal. I could tell she was going to be ready for riding before I would be if I didn't get my leg muscles prepared. So I went for a bicycle ride, with Duchess trotting alongside.

Milagro was bused home at noon. She skipped down the lane to home. When Joaquin got off the school bus that afternoon, he had a smile on his face. I was relieved that at least it was starting good.

My days took on an intensity. I swam in the mornings, increasing my time and distance, and biked in the evening as it was starting to cool. I spent lots of time grooming and lunging the horses. We were harvesting vegetables from the garden. I was eating them raw, steamed, baked, broiled, and stir-fried. I was also freezing corn on the cob, green beans, and peas. Sergio and I were trying to get a new coat of paint on the hay barn.

The oats had been harvested and the straw baled, but we still had a third cutting of hay to bale and bring in. I jokingly asked Cindy if she was going to help bring it in. She said yes and surprised me by showing up with Gage and Doug in tow. I had been happy all summer with the way my dream was fleshing out, but that assurance of help caused my heart to swell with gratitude to the point of tears.

I was beginning to wonder if the change of seasons would entice the snowy owl to migrate. I was hoping not. I wanted to ask Wee Shee what she thought as it seemed she was attracted to it as well. It seemed that whenever I noticed it, Wee Shee was close by, appearing after the owl flew away. Still, I wasn't comfortable talking to her, even though she had given me the bitter drink that had helped with my pain. I had thanked her for that, and she had responded with her dark-eyed stare. When I caught her watching me, I'd wave, but that too was answered with her trademark response.

Cindy came only on Saturdays and sometimes Sundays now. This particular weekend, we were going to the pasture to get Hobbit and Fancy to lunge them. Suddenly, Cindy's jaw dropped, and she gushed, "You rode Hobbit?"

"How did you know?"

"Fancy told me. She's jealous. She wants me to get on her."

"We don't have saddles and bridles yet."

"That's okay. She wants to do it bareback the way you and Hobbit did it; just around the pasture."

"All right. Let me give you a leg up."

I turned to look for Hobbit and saw her already standing by the gate. I grinned so wide I thought my face would crack. I clambered aboard again, no more graceful than the first time. We were expecting the rattling of the gate and so wasn't startled by it. The horses picked the pace, and I tried to cue Hobbit at the right times. It was enough to make us smile the rest of the day, no matter the fact that it rained.

We lunged the other two mares with Milagro and Joaquin aboard. Even the children helped groom them afterward. I was amazed that the horses' short summer hair was shedding out, already making room for their thicker cold-weather coats.

The nights were getting cooler. I decided that it was time to get the horses' blankets. I wondered if I'd find one small enough for Pip. In fact, I wasn't sure where the nearest equine equipment store might be. I didn't want to shop online. I preferred being able to see and feel the quality of what I was purchasing.

Once I had located the nearest store with Madison's help, Cindy and I measured for blankets, saddles, and bridles and then planned an all-day shopping excursion. After getting permission from her parents to make the two-hour trip, being sure Sergio knew we'd be gone all day, and assuring Duchess we'd be back, we hit the road.

The store was huge and had a wide range of quality and prices. The blankets, coolers, saddle pads, two- and three-step mounting blocks, and bareback pads were easy. Girths, irons, bridles, and saddles were much harder and might have to be returned.

I had the thought that there should be a store closer for at least the more common things that needed to be replaced frequently like blankets, fly masks, coolers, irons, girth sheaths, halters, and leads. The local feedstore had a small inventory of halters, leads, and fly masks; but the key word was *small*. I decided to figure up what size investment it would take to establish a store. I thought taking a small business course might be a wise move as well.

CHAPTER TWELVE

It was an overcast, cool Saturday on the second weekend of September. Cindy and I were lunging Nanny and Sugar when we heard the gravel crunching under tires. We heard Sergio asking if he could help and then saying "She's in the arena." It always amazed me how he could appear just as he was needed, always ready to step up to help with whatever transpired.

Sergio appeared at the huge doorway, followed by another form. I stopped Sugar and drew her to me. Taking hold of her halter, I walked toward the woman.

"May I help you?"

That was when I saw a small child with her arm around the woman's thigh. She had bouncy curls and thick glasses.

"Forgive me for barging in like this, but I need to find some place that takes boarders."

"I'm sorry. This isn't a boarding facility. There are a few places south and southeast of here."

"They're all full. I don't have time to wait on a list. Would you board just a pony? Dr. Kurt said you might."

The little girl was yanking on the woman's boot-cut jeans and pointing at Sugar.

"Would you like to pet her?" I asked, going down on one knee to get to her level.

The woman walked forward so the child could move with her without letting go of the death grip she had on the leg. Sugar accommodated by lowering her head to the child, who reached up and stroked Sugar's velvety nose. Sugar nuzzled the little girl's cheek, causing her to tuck her chin and giggle. And that drew a smile on the woman's face.

"I was right," she almost whispered.

"About little girls liking horses?" I asked, noticing a hearing aid in the small ear as well.

"Yes," she answered. "And that this is what Mindi needs to help her heal. I'm Sissy Black, by the way." She extended her hand to shake. Sugar reached her muzzle forward to sniff it. I waited my turn. The hand I then gripped was soft in the palm but firm in the clasp. The nails were short with crackle nail polish that matched the color on the child's small nails.

"I take it she doesn't have a pony now?"

"No. I thought it better to find a place to keep it first."

"I'll bet Pip would be perfect for her. Walk with us while we put these horses in the pasture. He's out there."

I was amazed at the rhythm Sissy and Mindi had established to be able to walk smoothly in their attached state. I couldn't help but smile even as my mind wondered what trauma little Mindi needed to heal from.

Pip was grazing close to the gate, waiting for Sugar and Nanny to return. He tried to push through the gate in his effort to get to them, but Sergio grabbed his halter and backed him up as we brought the mares through. Both horses nickered to the pony.

I knew Pip would want to go with the mares if we released them, so I continued to keep my hold on Sugar. Sergio kept his hold on Pip. Cindy shut the gate and released Nanny. It took Mindi a little while to realize there were two big dark eyes at a level she could actually look into. She stopped in amazement and then let go of Sissy's leg, walked up to Pip, and put her small arms around his neck.

Later that evening, after a soak in a hot tub, I was getting ready to sit down for a study session, but my mind wandered. Just five short months ago, I was wondering if I was ready to share my dream with anyone; and now my life was full of changes, people, horses, and sharing.

I had managed to squeeze into an evening small business class at the vocational school that would take up two nights a week. Cindy was now hitching a ride home with Elena to spend time exclusively with Fancy, and then I took her home on my way to class. The class gave me an excuse to go shopping for more clothes that fit my shrinking body.

Sissy was bringing Mindi to interact with Pip on Mondays, Wednesdays, and Fridays. Mindi always brought a small carrot or wedge of apple for Pip, and he was soon looking forward to his treat. They were usually there only half an hour, to begin with. It wasn't long, however, before we put Mindi up on Pip's back and led him around the mares. As the days cooled, we moved the sessions inside the arena. Pip resisted leaving the mares at first. He even occasionally gave a small buck that would unseat Mindi, who would giggle and ask Sissy to put her "back on . . . back on Pip." Mindi learned to cling like a burr to his back so those occasional bucks simply brought the familiar giggles without the accompanying unseating.

As she had watched us groom the other horses, Mindi was soon asking for a curry and brush. I didn't think she was ready for bridle and bit, so with Sissy's permission, we hooked snap-on reins to Pip's halter, put a stool in the arena, and turned Pip and Mindi loose. We took positions in opposite corners in case there was a problem.

For fifteen minutes, we watched as Mindi would carry the stool to Pip, who waited until she set it down before he would walk away. I could tell from my corner that Sissy was having as hard a time containing her laughter as I was. Finally, Mindi took Pip by the halter and led him alongside the stool where he stood until she stepped up onto it and was about to throw her leg over his back before he walked away. After a second time, Mindi stood with her little fists on her hips and scolded, "Pip, stop that."

She brought him back to the stool and again and wagged her finger in his face. "Stay."

And he did. We were afraid Pip would take it into his head to run, but that didn't happen the first couple of times Mindi rode on her own. And when he did finally run, Sissy and I both saw the extra kicks Mindi applied to the Pony's ribs urging him faster. She hung on laughing until Pip's tired legs forced him to slow and then stop. Mindi slid from his back and gave him a hug. "Good Pip."

—

The earth turned mellow. Goldenrod yellowed the roadsides; delicious yellow apples bent the limbs; the leaves were losing their deep green, though not yet turning color. The days were mild, followed by chilly nights. I was working Duchess on the agility course in the cooler evenings. She seemed to enjoy it more since the temperatures began to drop, and I needed a sweatshirt to stay warm. She looked like she had lost weight and was more toned from our agility work as well as our bicycle rides.

I was competing with the birds for the last of my harvest of berries. I had frozen lots of elderberries, blackberries, blueberries, and cherries. I had even made jelly from the blackberries and elderberries. Pies and cobbler had used fresh fruit. Pears, apples, and plums plucked from the tree were staples of our diets. I made applesauce and froze sliced apples. I made salsa from the tomatoes, onions, and green and red peppers. There was plenty for the family above the garage, and still the garden had not been picked bare. I sent stuff home with Cindy, and Sergio sent things home with their friends.

The pools were closed. The outbuildings and windbreaks had fresh coats of paint. The fields were empty, and the feed barns and freezers were full. I worried what I'd do with my time now. I'd have to discipline myself to sit at the computer and stand at the easel.

Sergio and I had arranged to alternate weekend chores so one or the other would actually get some time off. I would still go visit the horses, but I didn't help with scrubbing buckets and feed pans, with mucking stalls, or with feeding or walking the horses to and from the pasture.

I couldn't ignore the jealousy I felt over the help Sergio had when it was his turn. His wife and children helped make short work of the chores. But I was on my own unless Cindy showed up early enough to help. It was one of my turns in mid-October. As the horses ate breakfast, I broke the ice in the trough. It was supposed to be sunny and mild, so the panes of ice would melt over the course of the day. The horses got along in close proximity, so I was able to lead all four of them to the pasture at the same time. I didn't even need a lead on Pip. He kept close to the mares.

I was taking the feed pans and frozen water buckets to the garage, where warm water would help melt the ice and scrub them clean. Duchess barked, and I saw Doug's truck coming down the lane. I continued toward the garage, parked the wagon, and slid the door up on its tracks before I turned to him and said, "Good morning. What brings you out this way?"

"I thought I'd stop by and see how Pip is doing."

"He's in the pasture with the mares. They dote on him, but he's getting better at leaving them. He has a little friend that comes to love him and ride him."

"Really? How did you find the little friend?"

"It's more like they found us. You can go out and check on him if you want. I need to get these buckets and pans scrubbed."

"Okay. I'll be right back."

I scrubbed fast but still had only the feed pans done by the time he came back.

"They're all looking really good, even the mares. What are you doing?"

"Just TLC and making sure they're using their muscles."

"Well, it's paying off. Hey, where's Sergio?"

"We take turns having the weekend off."

"I see. What can I do to help?"

"You could rinse those pans."

"Okay. Uh, Madison wanted me to ask if you're interested in taking in boarders."

I kept my eyes on the water buckets as I contemplated the question. I could feel embarrassment coloring my face as I realized

I couldn't say yes. Was it just a short time ago that I was feeling isolated? And now I didn't want any more people in my space.

"I don't think so, Doug. I know that makes me sound selfish, but I think I like things the way they are. I'd be uncomfortable with a bunch of strangers around."

"They probably wouldn't be strangers for long, and it would be extra income."

I paused, contemplating it. "Do you have a personal friend looking for a place?"

"No. Madison's place has such a waiting list. She just thought if you were interested, she'd let you know there's a huge market for it."

"I'm more interested in having stalls available for rescues."

"Gage will appreciate that," he concluded.

I grinned. "I hope the rescues appreciate it more."

He grinned back. "No doubt. So what are you going to do the rest of the day?"

"I want to study my small business course notes. I have a good book in progress, and if Cindy shows up, we'll spend time with the horses."

"Next weekend is the Phoenix trail ride. Hopefully, next year, you'll have a horse to ride in it."

"Sounds like fun."

"Would you be interested in helping at the bonfire this year?"

"Doing what?"

"Cooking large amounts of food, setting up, pouring drinks, manning the grill, serving, whatever is necessary. We'd probably need you from about four in the afternoon until maybe midnight at the latest."

"Sure. I'm not sure where Phoenix is, though."

"I'll have Madison give you a call."

Cindy arrived soon after Doug left. Fancy and Hobbit indicated they were up for a ride. We did it the same way, except we used the two- and three-step mounting blocks to slip on their bare backs. We let them pick the pace, the route, and when they were done. We brushed them as they grazed. Then I let Cindy try her hand at guiding Duchess through the obstacle course, and later we invited Joaquin and Milagro over to play Cootie and Old Maid. I was amazed at how well they could both speak English. We all laughed and giggled our way through the games.

That evening, I got Madison's phone call. She told me what she needed. I told her what I could provide and that I could arrive at the needed time to help set up. I wasn't looking forward to it, but I wanted to foster their friendship and thought I'd better step outside my comfort zone to feed it.

CHAPTER THIRTEEN

The night of the trail ride turned out to be mild. The sky was just turning dim when I arrived at Phoenix. I had baked several dozen cut-out sugar cookies decorated with orange icing. I had pumpkin drop cookies and chocolate cupcakes. I had brought potato chips and buns for both hot dogs and hamburgers. Cindy had ridden with me and carried a Crock-Pot of baked beans. We transferred everything to a flat wagon covered in a layer of straw to cushion Crock-Pots and baking dishes. I could already smell all the different food. We all hopped aboard the wagons, sitting along the edges of the flatbed like crows perched on a fence.

Sitting next to me was a young woman who introduced herself as Arielle and her male companion as Jeremy. They managed a training facility abutting the back of Madison's boarding stables. She introduced me to several other people who were parents or spouses of others taking lessons or boarding at Phoenix.

"It's certainly a gorgeous evening for a trail ride," I offered. Everyone had to speak loudly to be heard over the growling of the tractor.

"Madison's trail rides always land on a beautiful evening," someone replied.

"Once, it snowed, but that only added to the charm. It wasn't cold enough to stick or enough to make the ground messy."

"How long have these trail rides been happening?" I asked.

"About six years now, I think. They've gotten so big I think she's going to have two next year: this one and another in mid or late spring. You can only go to one of them. She had to turn several people away this year. Only the first fifty RSVPs were accepted. They come from as far away as the East and West Coasts."

Another voice chimed in, "She has one on the Fourth of July also, but it's strictly for employees of the three farms."

"Three farms?" I gasped. "I had no idea she had such a huge operation."

"Well, the main farm, Phoenix, is the regular boarding stable. Lucky Deuces is the youth program. And Stepping High Farm is the training facility and show barn," offered Arielle.

"Actually," added Jeremy, "the show part and the training part will split within a few years if they keep growing as fast as they have been."

"Are you two going to tie the knot?" yelled someone from near the end of the trailer.

The two young people looked at each other and smiled, but neither answered the question. Jeremy did say, "It would make it easier if I didn't have to drive home every night."

Arielle gave Jeremy a punch in his arm. He laughed and put his arm around her. Then Arielle said, "We're thinking about doing it at the July Fourth trail ride."

The tractor and wagon had entered the woods. It was immediately darker. Young girls squealed in mock fright. I could see Cindy roll her eyes, but she kept her head down and didn't join in. We could still see the bright stars directly above us where the leaf tops didn't quite meet because the access lane had been cut through the trees.

It was a good while before we finally pulled into a cleared large area. There was already another group of men pulling picnic tables from a large shed with a garage-type door. The guys jumped down, headed straight for them, and began to help, setting them end to end near a shed off to the side of the several blackened fire rings. The men pulled several tarps from the huge pile of brush in the center of the area. Rain had been forecast for the past several days, none of which actually fell, and the tarps had been to keep the wood dry.

Arielle pulled a box across the straw. "Jillian, why don't you start by putting these vinyl covers on the picnic tables and then help set out the food? That shed is where the generator is, so the Crock-Pots needing electricity should be set on the table closest to it."

As I set about my work, I saw others filling the generator with gas. The kids were stacking seasoned wood in the darkened fire rings. Women took ropes from the shed and strung them from tree to tree as tie-lines. A man started one of the pit fires. One woman fired up the grill.

"We get to eat first," she explained. "What do you want: dog or burger?"

"Burger, please."

Shouts of burger, dog, and two dogs came from all over the area. Crock-Pots and coffee urns were plugged in.

Cindy appeared by my side. "See the dark-blue baking dishes? Those are what we get to eat from." She was pulling them forward, peeking under lids and foil coverings. There were baked beans, potato salad, salsa, hot and spicy cheese dips with corn chips, coleslaw, blueberry cobbler, and iced shrimp with a dip that everyone marveled about.

"I had to go one better than the crab cakes Arielle brought last year," explained a woman named Monica.

We all helped ourselves while waiting for the meat to cook. We filled our plates then and sat around the one small campfire while the others reminisced about previous trail rides.

"Jeremiah Johnson is sure to ask you to dance, Jillian, and it's okay. Part of our job is to help others have fun. But if he gets too pushy, you're allowed to say no," explained Arielle.

Someone else interjected, "Aw, he isn't pushy. He's just trying to be sure everyone has a good time. I think he's a real asset to the trail ride. He can really get the wallflowers to bloom."

"I agree. I was one of those wallflowers. He really helped me get beyond my shyness," came another unrecognized voice.

"He keeps trying to impress Madison."

"Yeah, well, I think she's got her eye on someone else."

I could feel my face flushing and was glad I'd be able to blame it on the fire's heat if anyone commented.

"Well, it's about time. It's been five or six years since Jake died. It's good to see love in her eyes again."

Someone's cell phone signaled a text. A moment of silence and then "Time to light the fires."

Several men set about the task. Some of the women went to stir the heating food, to make sure each container had a serving spoon, and to put meat on the grills.

We soon heard the snorts of the horses as they came from the dark, the fires reflecting from their dark eyes, making them look like demons from the ether world. Some of the horses threw their heads up and pranced as if defying the fires to keep them out of the clearing. The riders kept their mounts to the outer limits of the clearing, working around to the tie-lines. We could hear the riders murmuring as they loosened cinches, removed bridles, snapped leads to halters, reassured their horses, and as the night temperatures had significantly dropped, scurried to the warmth of the fires. From the fires, they converged on the hot drink urns.

Arielle called out, "Hot dogs and burgers ready," and the mob surged toward the food tables and queued at the grills.

I was standing out of the way, watching for how I might help.

"Hello. You're new here, aren't you?"

He was tall with gray at the temples. He sipped his steaming coffee while waiting for me to answer.

"Yes. I'm Jillian."

"You board at Phoenix?"

"No. I have my own place. I've just become friends with Madison and her staff, so they kind of recruited me to help out."

He extended his hand. "I'm Jeremiah Johnson. You live in Montaine, then?"

"No, I'm up around Clear Point."

"Do you have a stall you'd like to rent?"

"Sorry; I'm not a boarding facility."

His lips smiled, but there was sadness in his eyes. "Well, thanks anyway. How about a dance later?"

"I'm really sorry, but I'm not a dancer."

"You should change that."

"Maybe I will for next year."

"Next year is guaranteed to no one."

"You're right."

"So you'll dance with me?"

I laughed. "Probably not. I still can't dance this year."

"You're breaking my heart."

"I'll bet you won't lack for partners."

As Jeremiah moved toward the food lines, I caught a glimpse of Cindy slipping beyond the penumbra of firelight. I wondered if she was going to meet someone out in the dark. Was it safe? Should I follow? I stood indecisively, watching the spot where she had disappeared into the blackness.

The riders were gathering around the many fires, chatting and laughing, taking seats on the rough-hewn log benches. I heard someone giving training advice. Madison was circulating with a cup of hot chocolate in her hand, saying hello to everyone. I saw Doug coursing through the crowd. Jeremiah was sitting with a group of couples, and I spotted Gage sitting next to him, and next to Gage was a young man that looked very much like Gage. I wondered if Jeremiah knew Gage was his rival for Madison's affections. And was that young man related to Gage?

I filled a pot of coffee and one with hot chocolate then began circulating to refill cups. The pots were soon empty, and I went back to the urns to refill. Madison stopped to chat.

"How's it going, Jillian?"

"Okay, I think. I haven't done waitressing since I was in high school."

She laughed. "I really appreciate your help."

"No problem."

"I saw Jeremiah talking to you."

I bristled, wondering if Madison was the type that wouldn't want him but didn't want him to pursue anyone else either.

"You should take that as a compliment," she continued.

"How's that?"

"He's drawn to strong women. It's strange because then he wants to dominate them."

"How do you mean that?"

"Oh, order their meals or fill their plates without regard to what they might like; expect her life to revolve around his. Push his way into a life even if he's not wanted."

"Maybe he thinks the women are strong because they have to be, not because they want to be, and is trying to take some of the pressure off."

"I never thought of it that way."

"I didn't find him pushy at all."

"Well, I must say he's acting out of character tonight."

"By not being pushy?"

"He's kind of quiet. Usually he sits with a batch of older women or shy teens. He's always been able to get them to smile. I make sure he gets the first flyer. I think he really adds to the trail rides."

"Maybe someone has broken his heart."

She looked at me quizzically. "You might be right, of course, but I've seen him take rebuffs with a smile and bow out graciously before. And the wallflowers don't usually rebuff."

"Maybe this time was different."

"Could be."

"By the way, Madison, I saw a young person slip out into the dark. Should I go check on her?"

"I'll bet you mean Cindy." She laughed at the expression on my face. "She goes out to talk to the horses. She'll come back and let people know if their horses are having issues. Roger followed her out to be sure no one else bothers her. Hugh is guarding her right now. Margy will go out in just a bit."

"Oh, that's a relief. I didn't see the others go out."

"We try to be discrete. Before every event, we get together to assemble a 'Cindy team.' So if Cindy shows up, the team is already in place. It's nice of you to be concerned."

"I like Cindy."

"We all do. We're jealous that you get to see her more often than we do."

"I didn't steal her, you know."

Madison chortled. "Yes, we know, so we forgive you. We're really glad she found you. She really likes being around horses."

"Next year, hopefully, she'll be able to ride Fancy on the trail ride."

"That'll be great. She'll love that."

"I'd better get moving before these hot drinks aren't hot anymore."

"Thanks again for helping tonight."

As I made my way from fire to fire, cup to cup, I saw Madison lay her hand on Jeremiah's shoulder. He smiled up at her, but it didn't look like a happy smile to me. She sat next to Gage and chatted with everyone around that fire. She seemed to be trying to draw Jeremiah out, which I thought was cruel if she was whom he was pining over.

I saw Cindy come back to the group. She didn't look particularly happy either, but she didn't talk to anyone, so the horses must not have had issues. I was glad when two violins and a banjo appeared. Couples formed quickly, and Cindy grabbed Jeremiah's hand for a square dance. The violins continued with "A Soft Place to Fall." Jeremiah came to me.

"Just one dance."

"I'm so sorry. I really don't know how to dance." My face flamed red in embarrassment.

"Just sway to the music."

"I . . . I can't. I'd still be stepping on your toes."

"You really should remedy that."

"I will. I promise to dance with you next year."

He smiled, tipped his cowboy hat, and walked away.

Cloggers made an appearance. Doug came to chat while the rhythmic clomping filled the air. The line dancers took over. Jeremiah was up for one of those but then sat out the rest. I hadn't seen him too active in drawing anyone from the sidelines and wondered if he was the Jeremiah I had heard about all evening.

The dancing died out except for a few young people getting a clogging lesson on the dance floor. The fires were down to glowing coals. Empty food containers were being loaded back onto the flat wagons. People were scooping what was left, grabbing last bites of their favorite dishes. Others were gravitating toward the horses. We could hear the jangle of bridles being put back on, cinches being tightened, and horses stamping impatiently as we wiped off vinyl table covers. A breeze stirred the treetops and dropped down into the clearing to breathe new life into the embers and send sparks upward into the clear black sky.

Cindy found me and said she was riding back with Jeremiah on his horse and that she'd meet me there. As I had promised her mother to get her home safely, I told her it was fine; but when I saw Doug nearby, I asked him if he thought it was safe.

"Probably, but I'll be right behind them."

I sighed with relief and went about my business with occasional glances their way, trying to get a last glimpse of them before they disappeared down the trail into the night. I needn't have worked so hard at it. Jeremiah rode his horse through the clearing to where I was folding air-dried vinyl.

He tipped his hat. "Good evening to you, Jillian. It was a pleasure meeting you. Remember to take those dance lessons. Never know when you might need them."

"I will, Jeremiah."

He turned his horse toward the others already leaving. It was a handsome horse, lean and slim legged. Some lanterns had been turned on to give us light to work by as the fires were being extinguished, and I could see the bright white blaze and four white stockings, flaxen mane and tale against a chestnut body. *He must have a super name*, I thought to myself. If he saddled him with a name like George or Fred, I would have lost my respect for Jeremiah.

The wagon ride out of the woods is quieter than the earlier trip, I thought, until I heard whispered snippets of conversations— "Jeremiah not himself," "He was awful quiet," "Cindy riding with him. She must have a message from Sunset."

The wagons took a more direct route back to the parking area. I rounded up my cookie containers and then walked around the boarding barn and checked out the bulletin board. There were still plenty of horses in the stalls munching sweet-smelling flakes of hay, and a few were being ridden in the arena.

It was only about fifteen minutes before the first horses arrived. Owners eager to start for home had pressed their mounts for a faster pace and then dismounted, loosened girths, and led the horses the rest of the way to cool them out before loading into trailers. The others weren't far behind.

I saw Cindy slide from behind Jeremiah and head toward my car. I called to her, "Do you have your mom's Crock-Pot?"

"Yep," she replied, pivoted, and headed to the wagon to get it.

We were barely on the road before Cindy made her pitch.

"Jillian, are you going to rescue any more horses?"

"I imagine so. Why?"

"Sunset is going to need rescued."

"Who's Sunset?"

"Jeremiah's horse."

"Aah. He's already asked me to board him. I said no. I don't really want to board horses."

"But Jeremiah has cancer. Sunset is eighteen. He's had him fourteen of those years. He doesn't want to sell him. He wants someone to just take care of him."

"Eighteen isn't old for a horse. He could still be a good horse for someone. He'll get depressed if he doesn't have a purpose."

"Jeremiah knows that, but he says he doesn't have time or energy to find the right person for him. He said you can give him away or sell him to someone as long as they're a good match."

"Sounds like you've already got it figured out."

"Well, I know it's up to you, but Sunset is already sad because Jeremiah is dying."

I heard her sniff. "Is it really that serious?"

"Yes. He said he wasn't going to come on this trail ride, but he was hoping there'd be a new face . . . someone he could trust. He said he had a good feeling about you."

"Did you know Jeremiah was sick before tonight?"

"No. Sunset told me. He says Jeremiah talks to him all the time about how worried he is about finding him a good home."

"So you told Jeremiah you'd ask me?"

"No. I told Sunset you were pretty neat and I'd ask you to give him a home."

"How does he feel about that?"

"Like he doesn't have much choice. He's afraid Jeremiah will just give up if he isn't around to give him a reason to hang on."

"Poor guy." I choked, not knowing which poor guy I was talking about. Tears were filling my eyes, and the road blurred. "So how can I get hold of Jeremiah to tell him I've changed my mind?"

"Madison has everyone's phone number. But he was really tired. I think Sunset was spending the night in the quarantine stall and Jeremiah was staying at the motel on the outskirts of Montaine."

"Will we pass it on the way to Clear Point?"

"No. It's the other way."

"Well, I'll see if I can get hold of him when I get home."

Making the arrangements turned out easier than I had anticipated. Jeremiah's silver-and-gray horse trailer came down my lane at eight o'clock the next morning. I met him in the parking area.

"Jillian, thank you again for taking him in."

"Don't you want to keep him as long as possible? I can come get him when it's absolutely necessary."

"No. I've been worried sick about finding him a home. It's better this way."

"Please come visit him whenever you can."

"I might do that if you're sure it won't be a bother."

"Not at all. I'm going to go back inside so you can introduce him to the place, and visit as long as you like. His stall will be the third one on the right. There's hay and fresh water in the paddock. We'll keep him separated for a little while until he's more familiar with the other horses. And please *do* come visit him whenever you can."

"Thank you, Jillian."

I went back inside and watched from a window. If Sunset was beautiful by lantern light, he was stunning in sunlight. His coat was a bright sorrel with dapples declaring his health. His fine mane and tail looked strawberry blonde. He called to the mares, and they congregated at the pasture gate to check out the handsome new arrival. His head was up, ears pricked, but never a pull on the lead shank as Jeremiah led him into the stall row. He was in there a good while, but eventually, they emerged, and Sunset was put into the paddock.

They stood forehead to forehead, Jeremiah stroking his horse's neck. And then he unsnapped the lead from Sunset's halter and draped it over the gate, gave Sunset a hug around his neck, turned his back, and walked back to the truck. Tears ran down my face as I watched Sunset watch Jeremiah walk away. As the truck traveled down the lane, Sunset stood still and watched silently. The truck turned onto the road, and Sunset turned his body to watch it leave until it could no longer be seen. And still he stood, watching.

CHAPTER FOURTEEN

Early Monday morning, I awoke and lay listening. All was quiet. I should have added *peaceful*, but instead, my mind thought *ominous*. It was always quiet when I awoke. I knew it was only my concern for Sunset that made me feel differently about it now.

Duchess was already watching me from her bed, and when I threw back the covers and jumped up, she sprang from her own and paced while I quickly dressed. As I hurried toward the barn, I saw Sergio coming from that direction.

"He's okay but still sad," he said before I could ask.

It was while I was cleaning stalls that I began to wonder about relationships with animals. Were they all much deeper than people thought or just the occasional exceptional ones like Jeremiah and Sunset or Hobbit and me?

I leaned my four-pronged pitchfork against the stall wall and went to the end of the stall row to lean against the door jam and watch the horses. Hobbit immediately raised her head to look in my direction while chewing a mouthful of dried grass. Was she picking up my thoughts even from that distance? I walked toward the pasture gate, and she trotted toward me. I stroked her, hugged her, and thanked her for being mine—not just physically mine, but on a deeper level; and not mine as a possession, but mine as a friend, my fidus Achates. And I knew she knew what I meant.

I looked over at Sunset, who stood watching us. He had even quit chewing, the hay hanging from his mouth. Then he walked to the near side of his pile of hay, turned his whole body to face the other direction, and continued to eat. Was our relationship a painful reminder of what he had lost? Was watching our interaction actually causing him emotional pain?

I went back to my job and found Sergio mucking another stall.

"Sergio, it's my weekend."

"Si, but there is not so much to do. I will help again if our family has no plans."

"Okay. You can help when it's convenient for you."

As we finished our task, my mind started thinking of creating a story told from a horse's point of view. I decided to spend some time working on the idea when I got to the house. At about noon, I went to the kitchen for some fruit. I stood looking out the window at Sunset. He stood as if dozing. He looked so isolated and lonely.

"Stop it," I said out loud to myself. "You're projecting just because you know how isolation feels."

Yes, but I could do something about his.

I grabbed a lead on the way to the pasture and called Hobbit's name. She came at a canter. That was a first. She had trotted toward me before but never a canter. Did she sense what I wanted to do, and was she eager to accommodate me? Whatever the reason, it caused the other mares to throw their heads and dash to the gate as well. I had to push them back to get Hobbit out. I put her in with Sunset. I leaned against the pipe gate to be nearby in case of trouble. They were close in size. One was darker than a thundercloud; the other was as bright as a setting sun. Their winter coats were thick and unruly. They touched noses. There were no squeals or kicks to establish dominance. Hobbit wasn't, and Sunset didn't care.

The air was cold and damp. Even the house had a chill. I had brought in some kindling and logs, so I thought it was time to light the first fire. I needed a crackling blaze, a cup of hot tea, and time. I got out my small business notes to review. I played around with the horse story. I took a swim in my flowing-current pool and allowed Duchess to swim as well. I stood at the back door looking over the huge yard and realized the winter birds had arrived, and

I smiled to see them availing themselves of the leftover berries and seeds. I saw mountainous dark clouds surging across the sky.

Cindy arrived about one o'clock, chauffeured by her father. No sooner was he out the drive than Sissy and Mindi arrived. I left them alone to spend time with their mounts, and about an hour later, Sissy and Mindi left. Cindy came in slapping her gloved hands together, her cheeks and nose red from the cold.

"It's snowing," she announced with glee.

"Really?" I came through the foyer to the kitchen as she hung her coat. "Hot chocolate?"

"Yes, please."

"A game?"

"Yeah."

"Why don't you call Milagro and Joaquin to see if they can join us?"

I poured enough milk in the saucepan for all of us, got out four mugs and packets of hot chocolate, then stood staring out the window at the falling snow; big fluffy flakes were melting as soon as they hit the ground. I wondered if that counted as our first snow if there was no accumulation.

"Sergio says everyone is studying."

I put two of the mugs away. "Okay, why don't we make some pumpkin pies? We can play a game while they bake. Did you ask Sunset how he's doing?" I asked while we mixed pumpkin, spices, eggs, and milk.

"No," she answered in almost a whisper.

I looked at her in amazement.

"I'm sorry. I should have. I'm just afraid he's so sad I won't be able to handle it."

I went to her and wrapped my arms around her. "I'm sorry, Cindy. I never stopped to think how hard it must be on you shouldering the burdens of unhappy animals."

The fire had burned down to embers. I debated putting another log on the red coals. I had a book in my hands, and Cindy was doing homework.

"Snow always makes me want to go Christmas shopping."

Cindy's eyes lit up. "That sounds like fun."

"How about on the way home, you can help me pick out something for Joaquin and Milagro? And I noticed a moving van at a house down the road. How about we take them one of these pies on the way?"

—

As we pulled into the new family's home, the windows were ablaze with lights. Cindy carried the pumpkin pie. I rang the doorbell, and a little girl opened it.

"Hello. I'm Jillian Debaum. I live down the road. I saw the moving van here the other day. I brought you a pumpkin pie to welcome you to the neighborhood."

"Daddy!" yelled the little girl then turned back to me. "Do you live with the horses?"

"Yes, I do. Do you like horses?"

"Chelsea, quit being a bother. Hello, what can I do for you?"

"We just brought a pie to welcome you to the neighborhood. This is my friend Cindy. I'm Jillian Debaum."

"Wonderful, wonderful. I'm Reverend Aaron Davis. I'm taking over the Presbyterian church in Clear Point. I hope I'll see you in church this Sunday."

"Is your wife here?"

"My wife passed a few years ago."

"Trying to have my baby brother," piped in Chelsea.

"Chelsea, that's enough."

"But I have a big brother."

"Theo, come meet the neighbors," called the minister.

A sullen teen appeared in the room.

"This is Theophanous."

"Ted," insisted the boy.

"Do you like your new home, Chelsea?" I asked.

"No. I miss all my friends."

"Chelsea, we discussed that. You'll make new friends."

"Yes, Daddy."

"Well, here, we brought you a pie." Cindy handed it forward. Mr. Davis took it. "We need to get going. Have things to do." I looked directly at each of the children as I added, "Chelsea, Ted, I hope you both make new friends quickly. It must be very hard to have to make frequent moves."

It felt good to be back in the car. "I didn't pick up on too much happiness there. Did you, Cindy?"

"No. I've seen Ted in school the past week trying hard to prove a preacher's son doesn't have to be a good boy."

"Well, it can't be easy leaving friends behind . . . or being a preacher's son."

CHAPTER FIFTEEN

I should have introduced Sunset to the other mares one at a time as I originally planned, but the introduction to Hobbit went so smoothly that it gave me a false sense of security. I took Sunset to the pasture first and then all the mares at the same time as I usually did with Pip following on his own. Like an idiot, I had refused Sergio's help. To his credit, he followed close behind.

No sooner had I opened the gate than the mares rushed to the gelding, yanking leads from my hands and knocking me down. Hobbit had scrambled to get out of the way. Sergio was at my side in an instant.

"Are you okay?"

The squealing and thuds of flying hooves finding their mark had me on my feet. I started toward the plunging, spinning horses, their ears flat against their heads, teeth bared.

"No. You must let them sort it out. It is too dangerous now!" shouted Sergio above the ruckus, grabbing my arm.

I watched in horror as the leads flapped and swirled through the air. I worried that they would wrap around a striking leg, trip a horse, and cause it to break a leg or neck. Duchess circled the clump of fighting horses, barking as if trying to break up the fight, but staying a safe distance from the pulsing mass of equine bodies.

Finally, the clumps of dirt and brown grass quit flying through the air. Duchess quit barking. As she started back to me, Sunset made a last short dash at her with the devil in his eyes. Duchess dodged the snaking head, and then all the horses stood with heavy breaths, steaming in the cold air and looking like fire-breathing dragons.

"Oh my gosh. How could I have been so careless?"

"It's over now."

I stood immobilized in shock and shame while Sergio carefully went to each of the mares to unsnap their leads. I remembered that the gate was still hanging open. Pip was still on the other side of the fence, as if hiding from the fray. I used an apple wafer from my pocket to encourage him to come within arm's reach.

"Do you think it's safe for Pip to be in the field?"

"We'll keep a close eye on them today. I didn't see any blood or injuries that need tending. We'll look them over better when we bring them in this evening.

That seemed to be the end of it. Long ago, the hierarchy had been established. Fancy had the boss mare position, followed by Sugar and then Nanny. Hobbit seemed content to keep her distance on the bottom rung of the social order. When Pip came, he soon learned to make way for the mares also. Now Sunset revolved around the mares like a moon revolving around a clump of planets, as though he was not yet part of the hierarchy. Pip made forays toward Sunset, getting a little closer each time. Sunset ignored him. He only accepted Hobbit's nearness.

On my way to class that week, I stopped for a card to send to Cindy. She gave so much to others and the animals I wanted her to know she was thought of also. And our little shopping trip had gotten my mind whirling with ideas. I was sure Sergio and Elena wouldn't appreciate me purchasing a lot of gifts, but surely they couldn't complain to Santa! I had gotten Milagro a kaleidoscope and Joaquin a hundred-piece horse-picture jigsaw puzzle. I'd put my name on them. But I had also gotten a huge strap of bells and a large red velvet bag. I planned to pick up some clothes, toys, and books to wrap and fill the bag to leave outside their door. I was going to throw apples up on the roof to simulate reindeer noise and jangle the bells to announce Santa's presence. I thought of taking bites out of the apples to make it look like the reindeer did it. I was already grinning in anticipation.

When we had gone to the equine supply store, I had talked Cindy into trying on breeches, blouses, and boots. Then I took a picture with my cell phone. I told her to show her parents so they could see what she wanted. She sadly took them off, saying they couldn't afford anything so fine. But as she was hauling the equipment we had purchased out to the truck, I had gotten the items she had tried on and surreptitiously added it to our haul. I would need another velvet bag. Maybe I'd get her paddock boots to shift suspicion from me. I had a lot to do before Christmas.

Toward the end of the week, Jeremiah showed up with his brother as driver. Jeremiah barely looked his old self.

"Won't your brother get out of the truck?"

"Joel's too shy."

I went over to the truck and knocked on the window. He rolled it down, and I stuck my hand in to introduce myself. "Come on in for a cup of coffee, Joel. It's too cold to sit out here."

After a bit of chitchat over a cup of warmth, I asked, "Ready to go out to see him?"

"I don't know. He's doing good, right?"

"I think he's doing okay. He hasn't warmed to us yet, but he may still be grieving."

"Visiting him might just stir him up."

I didn't know what to say. It appeared to me that Sunset had been right. Without him, Jeremiah had no reason to hang on.

"Jillian, I really appreciate you taking him. Do you think you'll keep him or try to get rid of him?"

"Jeremiah, I would never just get rid of him. But I think he needs a job to do. A purpose, you know? The other horses have all been abused. He's had a good life with you and has many more years of service left. When the right opportunity arrives, we'll give him a new life. Until then, he'll stay here."

He got up to look out the kitchen window toward the pasture. "I knew I could trust you." He turned back to me with a sly grin. "Have you signed up for those dance lessons?"

"No, not yet." I grinned back. "Next session doesn't start until mid-January, so I have time."

I watched from the window as Joel went back to the truck and Jeremiah got a brush from the truck and went toward the pasture. He whistled and called the horse's name. Sunset called back with a loud whiny and galloped to meet him. Jeremiah stood next to his horse, grooming in long strokes. I could see his mouth moving as he spoke to his four-legged friend, and Sunset bobbed his head and turned it to look at the man as if answering him.

It appeared from my view that Jeremiah was tiring. His arm was slowing and finally stopped as he leaned against Sunset for support. I thought of getting him a folding lawn chair, but by the time I was emerging from the garage, Jeremiah was walking toward his truck, with Sunset watching his retreating back and then the truck as it went down the lane, down the road, and out of sight. I felt a stab in my heart for Sunset and then realized that this was the pain Cindy dealt with all the time.

I got home from small business class one evening, and Sergio came to say that I had a visitor. He was looking for a horse to purchase and a place to board it. Sergio had told him to return the following evening. I immediately felt trepidation. Why was I being asked so often to take in boarders? My mind immediately thought of how Sissy and Mindi had become part of our farm family by asking for a place to board and Sunset needing a new home. It seemed serendipitous, but I didn't feel I was ready or that Sunset was either.

I paced the house, picked up a book, and put it back down. Duchess followed me. I finally went down to the barn. I didn't turn on the lights. I went to Hobbit's stall and called her name. "Are you asleep?"

She whickered, and I smiled, wondering if she was answering "Not now."

I entered her stall, wrapped my arms around her neck, and leaned into her warm body. I couldn't stop thinking about the situation. I could feel myself getting defensive. Of course, I wanted Sunset to have a new owner, one that would appreciate him. I tried to convince myself that maybe a quick passage would be better than to have a long stay here and then make another switch. Or was it just me that didn't want to let go of him yet?

Hobbit threw up her head, breaking my grasp around her neck. Before I could ask "What's wrong?" or look for something that might have startled her, I heard a sharp voice in my mind admonish me: "Just say no."

I smiled, gave Hobbit a pat on her neck, and went back to the house.

The next day, I tried to keep busy to keep my mind off the man who wanted a horse and a stall. I swam, put Duchess through the agility course, lunged the horses—saving Nanny for when Milagro came home from morning preschool, and spent extra time with Sugar. She seemed to be falling through the cracks. Hobbit was special to me. Fancy had Cindy. Nanny had Milagro and Joaquin. Pip had Mindi. I realized I needed to give Sugar more of my time. I was sure Hobbit would understand.

Despite the sunshine, there was a nip in the air. I got a lap rug and went to the redwood swing to enjoy the view. I realized that there were a lot of birds around. They weren't chanting territorial mantras. That had disappeared in August. These calls sounded more like "This is a good place to winter."

The days were noticeably shorter. Dusk was approaching when the snowy owl dropped from the sky. She didn't bother to glance our way. After a moment, she mounted the air with a rodent clutched in her talons, arched through the sky, and disappeared on the far side of the apartment roof. I heard tires on gravel. I sighed, gathered up my lap rug, and went to meet the adversary.

He was a bit stoop shouldered, his salt-and-pepper hair just beginning to thin near the top of his head.

"May I help you?"

He turned from the door to face me. We were both speechless for a moment.

"Jillian?"

"Daniel?"

The young blond girl at his side took his hand, her blue eyes suspicious as she looked from me to Daniel.

"So you got your dream."

"I did." I couldn't help but grin smugly.

"Good for you. Jillian, this is my granddaughter, Sara. Sara, this is an old friend of mine. We went to school together."

So I had been relegated to old friend and classmate. I could feel a sneer forming on my face. I forced it away and replaced it with a smile. "Hello, Sara. What brings you here?"

I was looking at Sara and talking to her, but Daniel interrupted. "I'm looking for a horse for Sara."

"Do you live close by?"

"We live up in Drummond."

"That's a good distance to be driving every day."

"Well, it would be more a weekend activity."

I looked back at Sara. "Maybe you should just find a horse you can lease on shares. A weekend activity isn't being fair to the horse. How would you like it if your parents only took care of you on the weekends?"

"That's different," scowled the girl. "I'm only twelve, and I know that."

"Come on, Jillian. You have several horses and plenty of space."

"Being a boarding facility isn't what I want."

"You always were all about what you wanted."

"And now that I have what I wanted, you want me to let you use it?"

Daniel glared at me. "You're selfish, you know that?"

I thought of all the people, horses, and dog I was sharing my dream with. "Maybe, maybe not."

I saw Daniel force himself to soften his stance.

"Do you know anyone else with horses and space?"

I tried to relax a bit also. "No, Daniel. I'm actually pretty new to this area. I can give you the name of a riding center in Montaine."

"That big outfit? Phoenix, I think it's called. We've already been there."

"They have a youth program called Lucky Deuces."

"No, they want her there too often."

"Did you ask about a weekend lease?"

"No, she wants one of her own."

"She doesn't want one very bad if she doesn't want to spend more than a few hours on the weekend with it."

"Not everyone is as horse crazy as you are, Jillian."

"The horses need a little craziness."

CHAPTER SIXTEEN

The weather was acting like a yo-yo. One day it would be wet and cold, the next warm and dry. I had to check the weather before I could get dressed in the mornings, and I had actually used the fireplace twice already.

Thanksgiving was nearing. I wanted to ask Sergio if they wanted to have dinner with me, but I also didn't want to infringe on their own traditions as a tightly knit family. I settled for purchasing a turkey for them as a holiday bonus, gave them the week off to go visit family, and resigned myself to spending the day alone.

I was trying to be more disciplined in my activities—up at six o'clock to care for the horses, an hour of exercise, breakfast, two hours at the easel, free time until lunch, time with Duchess (the activity depending on the weather), time with the horses, a class, a book, a movie, company. Of course, it was all subject to shifts as circumstances dictated.

One night, at about ten, I was just crawling into bed when I heard a thump against the window. I turned just in time to see the snowy owl slide down past the windowsill. As I quickly slipped into my jeans, I wondered if the bird of prey kept diving into my window because she was retarded.

I dashed out the front door, around the side and stopped abruptly. There was Wee Shee walking around as though searching for something. She leaned over to pick something up.

"Did you see the owl hit my window?" I asked.

She looked at me, grinned as she brushed a white feather across the tip of her nose, winked, and walked past me toward her home above the garage. I was so stunned that I couldn't move—first, because she had actually smiled at me, and second, when she winked, I could have sworn that I saw the owl's face superimposed over hers.

When I finally regained my senses and turned to retrace my steps, I saw Sergio in the circle of light shed by the outside security light coming from the barn. I flattened myself against the corner of the house until he was up the stairs and inside the apartment. *Now why had I done that?* I wondered. *What was wrong with just asking if he was checking on the horses?*

As I crawled back into bed, I remembered the last time the owl had collided with my window. Sergio's truck wouldn't start, and Elena needed a ride to her class. *Was the owl acting as a messenger?* As I drifted off to sleep, I thought about how whenever I saw the snowy owl, I soon after saw Wee Shee. There must be a connection somewhere.

It snowed a couple of inches overnight. On my way to the barn, I saw Sergio's footprints in the snow leading to the stalls. It dawned on me that since Sunset had arrived, Sergio was usually grooming him when I arrived for the morning feedings. Things had certainly changed. I remembered when Sergio and I would meet as we were both coming for the first feeding of the day. I wondered if he thought Sunset needed some extra TLC or if there was more to it than that.

Sergio put Sunset back in his stall. As we began distributing flakes of hay, I asked, "Sergio, have you thought of what you're going to go to school for? Elena is halfway through hers."

"Si. Mr. Frank suggested welding."

"That would be a good choice. You don't sound sure that's what you want."

There was no immediate answer. I turned to look at him. "Sergio?"

He shrugged his shoulders as he continued to work with his head down.

"Sergio, it's okay to disagree with your mentor. Is there something else you would prefer to do?"

He answered so softly I could barely hear his words.

"I like it here very much. My family have always been farmers, and I love the horses."

I smiled. "Ah, I know how you feel. But what has that to do with it?"

"Mr. Frank says, after we get our educations, we are to move on to better jobs and make way for others to work."

"I see. What if I don't want to let you go after you get your education?"

He didn't look up as he was measuring grain into the feed pans, but I saw a smile tug at the corners of his mouth.

"Sergio, I think welding would be a good skill to have. I'm sure you can use it here on the farm as well as other places if you ever decide to move on. You'll be more marketable if things change, and you know things always change."

"You will not make us leave?"

"No. In fact, I will be very happy if you stay. I am very pleased with your work."

He looked at me then. "I have another wish."

"What's that?"

"I want to buy Sunset from you."

"No."

His face went slack.

"He was given to me to guide him into a new life. So I give him to you."

His eyes widened in shock.

"All I ask is that if you can't care for him at any point, you give him back as opposed to selling him."

A grin grew wide on his face. "Si, si. Gracias. Bless you. Bless you."

"So don't forget to sign up for welding classes."

"Si, si."

But his mind was far from welding that day. When I went to lunge the mares, Sergio was riding Sunset in the arena. I hadn't even asked if he knew how to ride, but he looked as if he had been doing it most of his life.

—

I couldn't hear the phone ring from the exercise room, and I refused to answer it when I'm painting or writing. So by the time I checked for messages that evening, there were several on the machine. The first three were from Daniel, the fourth from Cindy.

"Why haven't you returned my calls?" shouted Daniel.

"I'm returning it now."

"I've been calling all day."

"Daniel, I have a life. I don't sit by the phone waiting for people to call. That's what answering machines are for. What can I do for you?"

"I want to ask again to buy or lease one of those horses."

"I'm sorry. All the horses here have caretakers."

"What about the big red one?"

"First, he would be way too much horse for Sara. And second, he has a new owner."

"You were avoiding me, weren't you? Just so you could tell me no."

"Daniel, I'm going to hang up now. The horse is not available, so we have nothing to discuss."

"You have other horses there."

"They aren't for sale or lease. Goodbye, Daniel." I hung up softly and quickly dialed Cindy's number. "What's up, Cindy?"

"My parents want to know if you'll come for Thanksgiving."

"Thank you. I'd love to. What time?"

"I thought I'd come out in the morning about ten. Then we can come back here about three. Dinner is at five."

"Sounds good. Thank your parents for the invitation."

"Okay. See you this weekend."

No sooner had I hung up than the phone rang again beneath my hand.

"Jillian, how about having dinner with me?"

"No, Daniel. Things haven't changed between us, and you won't get a horse that way either."

"You haven't changed."

I forced myself to answer softly. "I'm going to hang up now. Please don't call me again. We have nothing to say to each other." I hung up the receiver as gently as my tense arm could manage.

It rang again.

"Daniel, I said not to call gain."

"This is Jeremiah."

"Oh, I'm so sorry. What can I do for you, Jeremiah?"

"I wanted to come visit Sunset next week. Since there's a holiday, I thought I'd better check with you instead of just showing up."

"Thanksgiving Day is going to be busy, but you could come the day before or the day after." I thought of Cindy being here on Friday. "Actually, Wednesday would be the better day."

"Wednesday it is. See you then."

Although the night temperatures stayed below freezing, the snow melted by noon on Wednesday. Sissy and Mindi arrived as I finished lunging Hobbit and was putting her back into the paddock, which was our sacrifice area. Mindi took a lead and walked bravely to retrieve Pip. The little pony did his part by coming to her call. I was amazed at the difference in her, from the child that had clung to Sissy's pant leg to going alone into the paddock among the big horses.

Sissy and I were both standing at the gate, watching her confidently greet her friend.

"Jillian, I'd like to invite you to Thanksgiving dinner."

"Oh, Sissy, that's so nice of you, but I've already accepted another invitation."

"What about Christmas dinner then?"

"That would be wonderful."

"That's settled then. It's our way of thanking you for helping Mindi."

"All I did was allow two hurt souls to heal each other."

"Yes . . . and thank you."

"Say, how would you like to baby a horse since you're here anyway?"

"What do you mean by baby it?"

"Brush her, lunge her, at some point ride her. It could become a mother-daughter activity."

"Is she gentle? Even though I knew a horse would help Mindi, I'm actually afraid of them. They're so big."

"Let me bring Sugar in and introduce the two of you."

I put Sugar in the crossties, handed Sissy a brush, and instructed her to brush with the lay of the hairs.

As involved as Mindi was with Pip, her eyes grew large and round when she saw Sissy grooming the light bay.

"Are you going to ride too, Mommy?"

Sissy dropped the brush as both her hands rushed to cover her mouth. Then with tears in her eyes, she knelt next to Mindi. "Would you like that?"

Mindi nodded her head enthusiastically and then went back to brushing Pip.

Sissy returned to Sugar and, through her tears, explained, "That's the first time she's spoken directly to me or called me Mommy."

"I always assumed you weren't her biological mother."

"No." She lowered her voice. "She was in the foster care system, and a foster brother raped her about a year ago. My husband, Dylan, and I adopted her."

"That was brave. She'll probably have psychological problems all her life."

"Not if we can give her enough good relationships to squeeze out the bad memories."

"Now you have to learn to ride. We'll start today."

"I don't know about that."

"Just at a walk. You'll be fine."

I got a bareback pad from the tack room and adjusted the stirrup length for Sissy's long legs. Sugar stood still as Sissy mounted up and was well-behaved as she circled me on the lunge line. Occasionally, we noticed Mindi and Pip standing quietly in the corner, watching.

"Sissy, sit up straight. Let your pelvis move with Sugar's steps."

"I feel like I'm going to fall off."

"That's because you're stiff. Breathe. Pretend Sugar is a feather mattress. Let your body sink into her, but keep it upright."

"Look at her ears moving. Am I making her angry?"

"No, she's listening to you."

"But I haven't said anything."

"You're speaking with your body; your relaxing or tensing; weight shifts; squeezing hands or legs—they're all used to let the horse know what we want of them. Sugar is trying to figure out what you want her to do. After you learn to hold your seat and be consistent with your cues, she'll understand you better."

"I didn't realize there was so much to riding a horse."

"There's nothing greater than riding a well-trained horse."

We kept the lesson to twenty minutes, but even so, Sugar was warm with the unaccustomed work, and Sissy's thigh muscles were sore. Sissy had barely turned their car onto the main road before I saw Jeremiah's truck pull in. By the time I got to the vehicle, Joel had gotten a wheelchair from under the cap and helped Jeremiah into it. I was shocked at how much he had deteriorated. I couldn't bring myself to ask the usual question of how he was.

"Jeremiah, you look tired. Long drive?"

"Everything tires me these days."

"Joel, nice to see you again."

"And you." He smiled.

"How's my boy doing?"

"Good. Real good."

Joel was pushing him toward the paddock gate. I saw Jeremiah take deep breaths and then let out a whistle that belied his frailty. I saw Sunset's head shoot up, pause, and drop again. I heard Jeremiah's breath catch in his throat.

"Try again," encouraged Joel.

"No. He heard. He chose. Let's go. Jillian, I thank you."

I took his hand and squeezed. What could I say? "Take care of yourself, see you later, get well soon, I'm sorry"? I held his hand all the way to the truck. When he stood to get into the cab, I gave him a hug.

"He's ready to move on, Jillian."

I only nodded. I watched Sunset as the truck went down the drive, down the road, and out of sight. He kept his nose to the ground, not once lifting it to watch his friend leave for the last time.

CHAPTER SEVENTEEN

On Thanksgiving morning, all the horses were saddled with bareback pads and in use at the same time. Mindi was kicking Pip, urging him faster, but he maintained his herd manners. I sidled up next to Sissy and explained how a rushing pony might startle one or more of the horses, causing them to kick out. Although Pip was not tearing around as Mindi was encouraging him, I felt Sissy should explain to Mindi why she shouldn't urge the pony to rush around.

I held the reins while Sissy got down from Sugar's back and explained to the sensitive child. Mindi cried a little but then let Pip keep close to Sugar. That satisfied Mindi as Pip had to trot to keep up with the Thoroughbred.

Joaquin and Milagro were riding double on Nanny. Sissy on Sugar kept close to Hobbit. I'm sure it was because she was still unsure of herself and wanted to be close to me in case she had trouble getting Sugar to go where Sissy wanted her to go. Hobbit worked as a buffer between the dominant mares and Sunset, although Sergio was handling him expertly. His hands were soft on the reins. Sunset's ears swiveled, listening for every message Sergio might send. Fancy, of course, thought she should be in the lead as boss mare. I had to give Cindy credit for making her mind. She would make Fancy follow the group or move alongside the group, even brought her up between Nanny and Sugar, and then, as a reward for doing well, let her take the lead for a while.

It made me feel good to see all my rescued horses adding dimension to so many lives. No matter what Daniel said, I knew I wasn't selfish. I was just picky about whom I shared with. Maybe I just didn't want to cast my pearls before swine.

It was snowing again. The high for the day was supposed to be twenty-eight degrees but not windy. I wanted to give the horses a chance to get some fresh air, so I decided to put the horses in the paddock without their blankets, but we would also bring them in early.

The agility equipment had been put away for the winter, so Duchess was getting outside exercise only if the kids wanted her to come out to play in the snow. I was making sure she got swim time. I even tried getting her on the treadmill. It took a few tries, but she finally accepted it. And today, Cindy walked alongside her, which made Duchess happy.

Even though I had been invited away for dinner, I had made a small turkey stuffed with dressing for myself, just so I'd have leftovers to eat for a couple days. *Leftovers are one of the perks of the holiday*, I thought. When I got back to the house, I could smell my turkey roasting. Cindy asked if I wasn't coming to her place after all. I laughed and explained my desire for leftovers.

I saw the blinking light on the answering machine. I felt dread, thinking it might be Daniel. But it was Doug, and I happily returned his call.

"What are you doing for dinner?" he asked.

"Cindy's family invited me."

"That's good."

"What about you?"

"Vickie Torrence invited me to spend it with her family."

"That's nice. I'm glad you won't be alone. Interested in leftovers tomorrow?"

"Sure, but I thought you said you were dining out."

"I still made myself a bird so I'd have leftovers."

"Smart gal. Sure. I'll come. What time?"

"About one?"

"That works for me. See you then."

Cindy was grinning.

"What?"

"He likes you."

"He's just being nice."

"By inviting himself for leftovers?"

"I invited him."

"You called and invited him?"

I was speechless. "Are you ready to go home, smarty-pants?"

"Yep. By the way, Sunset really likes Sergio."

"I'm glad. He wouldn't come to Jeremiah yesterday."

"I know. He told me. He said it was all he could do not to, but he didn't want to feel that abandonment when Jeremiah left again. Sunset said it still hurts."

"I'm so sorry. Does he think Sergio will help him forget?"

"No. But Sergio will help him accept that things change."

It was still snowing Friday morning. Sergio rode Sunset, and I rode Hobbit early and put them back in their stalls. The temperatures were supposed to drop and usher in more snow. Everyone else showed up about ten o'clock, including Doug.

"I wanted to see how everyone was doing," he explained with a grin as he tweaked Cindy's nose.

He was amazed as Joaquin and Milagro used step stools on either side of Nanny to groom and saddle her and also at the ease with which Mindi handled Pip. Sissy seemed a little more confident on Sugar and tried to not follow the other mares so much but made a game of following Pip and Mindi. Doug, Sergio, and I sat in the observation booth, enjoying the show.

"What are you smiling about?" questioned Doug.

"Oh, just all these people and all these horses enjoying themselves; the snow, leftovers waiting for us; a warm house; friends. It would be hard to ruin today."

As the horses were put back in their stalls, Cindy slid next to me and put her arm around my waist. "Sissy is going to take me home. I've got some homework to do."

"Are you sure?"

"Yeah."

"Will you be here tomorrow and Sunday?"

"Yes, but I think the horses need a break from us riding them."

"Okay. Do you want me to come get you early? We could go out for breakfast."

"I'd like that."

Doug and I meandered to the house.

"How was dinner at Vickie's?"

"The meal was great. She has a teenage daughter that is a master in the kitchen. She's actually interested in becoming a chef. Bill and I watched the game."

"Did your team win?"

"Of course."

The answering machine was blinking. I felt the familiar dread of talking to Daniel, so I ignored it. Doug and I played Scrabble and watched a movie. He looked over my shelves and asked to borrow a book.

"That'll give me a reason to stop back," he said without looking at me but leafing through the pages.

"You don't need a book as an excuse to stop back. You're welcome anytime."

"Well, thank you. Care to take in a movie?"

"Which one? I'm kinda picky about what I watch."

"I'll give you a call next Friday afternoon to discuss what's showing. We'll grab dinner before. Is that okay?"

"Sounds good to me. Casual okay?"

"Yep. Thanks for sharing your day with me."

"Anytime."

I saw him to the door. He reached down to give Duchess a rough head scratch. She looked up at him soulfully as he scratched behind her ears. He looked back at me. "See you next Friday."

"Looking forward to it."

As I closed the door against the cold, the phone rang. I was pretty sure it wasn't Doug, so I let the machine pick it up.

"Jillian, this is Madison. You don't have to do it," she growled. Disconnect.

Do what? I wondered. *What was she so angry about?*

The phone rang again, and I picked it up. "Jillian, this is Gage. I have a severe abuse case."

"Are you pulling in the drive?" I asked, grinning.

"No."

I didn't hear any amusement in his voice at my jest.

"Jillian, to be honest, I figure this gal just needs a place to die."

I sobered up immediately as thoughts of the gray and Sunny flashed through my mind. Tears instantly sprang to my burning eyes. "That's my specialty," I croaked.

He heard the crack in my voice. "You're allowed to say no."

"If I wanted to say no, I would, but you know how I feel about the hopeless cases."

"They all deserve a chance."

"That's right, even if it's just the chance to die sheltered."

"Jillian, I'm really sorry to do this to you. She may not be alive by the time I get there, but I just couldn't leave her there. Madison was with me and wanted to put her down." He paused. "I just couldn't let her do it even though it would probably have been the humane thing to do."

"And she's angry because you wouldn't let her."

"Boy, is she ever."

I could hear the sadness in his voice and wondered how my statement that they all deserved a chance overrode his desire for a relationship with Madison. It sounded like it had created a major rift.

"Any disease I need to quarantine her for, or is it just neglect?"

"More than neglect. Physical abuse. She has a lot of scars from whipping, it looks like. I imagine hopelessness is one of the reasons she may not make it. She's so far gone Madison wouldn't even examine her. Just wanted to put her down. She's been out in this weather; wheezing really bad; could be pneumonia."

"What's your ETA?"

"Travel time is an hour. Depends on how long it takes to get her loaded. Madison left, so I'll be working alone."

"I'm sorry, Gage."

"For what?"

"Causing this tension between you and Madison."

"Number one, you didn't cause anything. Number two, no pressure, but you'll just have to pull her through so we can say 'Told you so.'" Finally, I heard a smile in his voice.

"I'll have a stall and a warm mash ready."

"She probably won't eat."

"That'll be her choice. Just get her here."

When I hung up, I saw the machine still blinking from the earlier ignored message. I hit the Play button. "Jillian, this is Joel Johnson. Just wanted to let you know Jeremiah died on Thanksgiving Day. His last words were 'Tell Jillian to dance.'"

I made my way to the barn to get the stall ready with tears freezing on my cheeks. Sergio was coming down the stairs, and again I wondered how he could appear at just the right times and then realized that it was time to feed the horses.

The temperature had dropped as promised, and the snow was coming down in huge flakes. I told Sergio about the mare coming. He began feeding as I got the stall ready. I put hot water in the water bucket, knowing it would be tepid by the time Gage got here. I put mash in a clean feed pan but no water. I wanted it to be fresh.

We had checked hooves and finished a quick brush on the horses when we heard Gage pull in. Sergio opened the sliding door to the stall row and guided Gage as he backed the trailer in close to the stall door. I opened the trailer door as he came around to the back. The horse was down. Gage jumped into the trailer to check for signs of life. No one said a word as he came back out, closed the trailer, and drove away.

CHAPTER EIGHTEEN

The following week seemed quiet after all the turmoil over Thanksgiving. It snowed all weekend. Sergio, with Joaquin sitting between his legs on the tractor seat, his small gloved hands on the steering wheel next to his dad's, did a good job of keeping the lane and parking area cleared.

The events of Friday night had me feeling blue. I was spending all my barn time with Hobbit. Cindy and Sergio picked up my slack without complaint. I told Cindy about Jeremiah's passing. She must have relayed it to Sunset as when we turned the horses into the arena for indoor exercise, he stood off alone, not even interested in his flake of hay.

I went to the barn a couple of times just to be with Hobbit and to absorb the strength and comfort she always seemed to exude. Standing there with my arms about her neck and her head hanging over my shoulder, I thought I heard "You can't save us all." Still, it made me sad that the last one didn't realize she was going to be given the opportunity to live before she died.

On one of the times I went to the barn, Sergio was brushing Sunset, trying to cheer him up, I was sure.

What a sad bunch we are, I thought.

Jeremiah's last words popped into my mind: "Tell Jillian to dance." It occurred to me that I could take that beyond the literal meaning of taking dance lessons to engaging in life to the fullest. I remembered the Souza saying "Dance as though no one is watching you. Love as though you have never been hurt before. Sing as though no one can hear you. Live as though heaven is on earth." I was determined to try.

I used my trips to my small business class to continue my Christmas shopping in Drummond. It was so bitter cold on Wednesday morning that Sissy and Mindi didn't even come. By noon, the temperatures warmed. The snow on the roofs dripped into icicles, and on the ground, it settled into a moist pack that squelched under footsteps and rolled into wonderfully strong snowmen.

Duchess and I utilized the current pool and treadmill to keep active. I had a painting in progress, spent time each day writing my stories, reading, or sitting with a hot drink near a window to watch it snow or the sun glint off the white ground cover, making it so bright I had to squint.

I felt so grateful for my dream come true, the warmth of my home, the comfort of a fire in the hearth, the friends that had come into my life, and Duchess always by my side.

—

On Thursday morning, I had just finished drying the breakfast dishes when the phone rang. "Hello?"

"Jillian, this is Daniel. How about having dinner with me?"

"Daniel, I'm really sorry, but I have no desire to have another relationship with you. We've been there, done that."

There was only the sound of him softly hanging up. I almost felt bad for him, but at the same time, I hoped his silence meant he finally accepted the futility of his efforts.

As I stood at the kitchen window staring across the parking area at the horses in the pasture dressed in their blankets pawing at the heavy snow covering the brown winter grass, the snowy owl swooped through the air to land on the peak of the garage apartment. As I watched, it seemed to stare back at me. My skin prickled as the dark eyes seemed so like Wee Shee's even from this distance. I had looked up the bird in a field guide when it first appeared long ago to discover it had amber eyes. But these eyes staring back at me were black and so familiar.

The phone rang. I stood near it but let the machine answer. "Jillian, this is Doug."

I snatched up the receiver. "Hi. What's up?"

I was wondering if you'd like to take in a play and have dinner with me."

"Sure. When?"

"Tomorrow evening. There's a theater and a great place to eat in Damascus called Diamonds. It's a black tie. Ritzy place."

"Sounds nice."

"It's about a two-and-a-half-hour drive, so I'll pick you up about four."

"I'll be ready."

"See you then."

I felt an excitement I had never felt before. I knew I needed to keep busy, but no matter what I did to occupy my mind and hands, my thoughts wandered back to my date with Doug.

I wore black from head to toe, including onyx and diamond earrings and an inch-wide black velvet choker. When Doug arrived, I saw his eyes go to the choker.

"You said black tie, right?"

"That I did," he conceded.

He was wearing a black suit, white shirt, and black tie. I wondered if the restaurant would be full of penguin-looking men or if Doug was just a bit unimaginative.

"So how did you land in Clear Point?" he asked.

"Via moving van."

"Let's start again. Where did you start from?"

"Born and raised in Indiana. Parents were both teachers. I was an only child. I think they had me just because they thought that was expected. Not sure they really wanted a child. I didn't know there was such a thing as grandparents until I got to school and was left sitting alone on Grandparents' Day."

"Wow. Your parents had no pictures or ever mentioned their own parents?"

"Nope. When I asked, they both said they were orphans. They met in an orphanage; had to leave it when they turned eighteen, so they left together just so they each wouldn't be alone. They both got jobs, got married because they were afraid of repercussions if they just lived together. They worked their way through college, lived very frugally, got their teaching degrees, got jobs at the same school. Mom taught first grade, and Dad high school. The most attention I got from them was how to be a good student. By the time I was six, I was ready for third grade. But back then, they didn't move kids ahead. So I was really bored at school. It was at home that my parents kept furthering my education. Going to school was more to keep me off the streets while they were at school teaching. Once I reached fourteen, I was permitted to be exclusively homeschooled. So I was out shoveling snow, pet sitting, lied about my age to get a waitress job. That was the only way I could get the money for anything I really wanted that wasn't a necessity. When I turned eighteen, they barely noticed when I went off to college. I tested out of all the first- and second-year English and math courses. Became a nurse. Not sure when I knew I wanted a farm to have horses, but all my focus and efforts have been to that end since then."

"And you succeeded."

"Yes, I did."

"But . . . ?"

"But at what cost? Somewhere along the line, I never learned to be social."

"I don't see how you could have been a nurse without being socialized."

"Oh, I knew how to converse, just not how to have relationships. I never had a best friend; never went shopping or to the movies with a gaggle of girls."

"You never married?"

"Yes. I guess I thought married I wouldn't be so alone, but I still was. We had different goals. He was living in the present, and I was still focused on a future horse farm."

"Would you do it differently if you could go back?"

I paused, thinking about when I first moved into my dream. "At first, I wondered if I'd been wrong, but look at the people and horses in my life now." I smiled. "Now, it was worth every step of the journey."

"Do you visit or call your parents?"

"They both died soon after they retired from teaching. I don't think they saw anything worth living for after that." I paused again. "That's sad, isn't it? Orphaned, forced to leave the only place they felt any safety; struggling to get an education. I wonder if they enjoyed teaching."

"They must have if they came home from teaching jobs to teach you."

"Yes, I suppose so. But I don't recall ever seeing them smile or argue. I don't recall visits to neighbors. I have no idea what went on behind closed doors. Did they learn to love each other?"

"That was quite a journey."

"How much is luck? How they met, what they did to survive. And in my life, the jobs I found and worked; why did my farm become available before the others I had my eye on?"

"Boy, that could be a deep conversation."

"Well, let's not go into it. What about you? What's your story?"

"Knew all four grandparents. They were all very loving. I spent at least a week at each home over the summer. I have three brothers, no sisters. Dad passed a few years ago. Mom is still living with my youngest brother and his wife, Libby, in California. He's an ear, nose, and throat doctor. Mom and Libby always had a special relationship even back when Josh was dating Libby. My older brother Derrick and his wife, Connie, also live on the West Coast. He's an orthodontist. Jared and I are the confirmed bachelors. Jared is a tax lawyer in Texas."

"Why is Jared in Texas?"

"Big oil money in Texas."

"And how did you come to be on the east side of the Mississippi?"

"Well, I always thought there was something missing . . . like green grass. Maybe I was a cow in a previous life." He laughed. "I had actually retired. Bought a Winnebago to travel and see the country. But I got restless. As I was passing through Montaine, I went into Madison's clinic and asked for an application. And frankly, this is the first I've really felt like I was home."

We were passing through a rural stretch with no streetlights. I felt it was safe to chance a smile.

CHAPTER NINETEEN

It was one in the morning when we turned into my lane.

"It's so late. I almost feel guilty for sending you home."

"Is that an invitation to stay?" His grin glowed in the shine of the security lights.

I paused for a second. It had certainly been a long time since I had experienced a man. "No. That isn't an invitation. Just an admonition to be careful going home."

"Is that a sign I can hope?"

I grinned back, but that was when I noticed the barn lights were on. "Doug, would you drive closer to the stables? I want to check who's in the barn."

His smile died also. "Maybe it's just Sergio, but give me a head start to check for trouble. Then you can come in to check if anything is missing."

I waited until he disappeared through the open door and then followed, my small pumps sinking in the soft, moist snow. He was halfway down the aisle looking in each of the stalls. The sliding door at the far end of the aisle was open about eighteen inches. The tack room door was open. Pip's stall door was open, and only one corner of the stall guard was hooked. A brush was on the floor outside the pony's stall.

Doug was peering out the open door. "Looks like tracks. I'll follow them. Stay here."

I put things back in order, checked the tack room for anything missing, went to Hobbit to ease my worry and listen to the horses munching grain someone had put in their feed pans.

"The tracks lead straight across the front field. The road is clear, so of course, I can't tell which way they went," said Doug as he came in, stomping the snow off his black dress shoes and sliding the door shut behind him. "Maybe you should install an alarm system."

I was stroking Hobbit's jowl as she breathed her warm horse breath smelling of sweet feed on my face. I thought for a moment. "The horses don't look startled. Except for getting an extra ration of food, there's no harm done. Looks like they just wanted to groom a pony."

"Maybe making friends so they're easier to load."

"Ah, you have a point. But first, I'll just put locks on the feed and tack rooms. Then I'll start barn checks during the night, see if we can catch the culprit."

"Plural. There are two sets of tracks: big boots and small boots."

"Do you think they'll be back tonight?"

"I don't know. Maybe we scared them. Maybe they're just waiting for the lights to go off."

"Well, I'll check again in a couple hours."

"Be careful."

"I will."

I set my alarm for three o'clock and again for seven thirty. The barn was dark and void of intruders at three. Duchess accompanied me and sniffed all along the aisle. At seven thirty, I phoned Sergio. "Sergio, I had a late night last night. Can you handle the chores this morning?"

"Si."

"And we had visitors in the barn last night. Skip the horses' grain as I don't know how much they got fed by the intruders. Give extra hay. And I want you to put padlocks on the feed and tack rooms today."

"Si."

"We're going to have to start checking the barn at different times of the night for a while, see if we can catch whoever it was."

"Si."

"Okay, I'll talk to you later."

My eyes opened to bright sunlight. The clock showed that it was noon on the dot. I couldn't believe I had slept so long and so deep. I quickly got dressed and put on my coveralls and barn boots. Duchess was bright-eyed; her stubby tail vibrated, causing her whole backside to wag violently. She seemed to be saying, "What took you so long? What's up for today? Come on, we're late."

I wanted to brush Hobbit, but the horses were in the pasture without their blankets. It was a lot warmer, and the snow wasn't as deep as it had been the previous night. It was too warm for the coveralls. I went into the stall row. The padlocks were installed. Two keys were hanging on a nail nearby each. I was just about to take one key and leave the other for Sergio when he walked through the doorway.

"Those are for you, senora. I kept one already. You should keep one for a spare."

"Thanks, Sergio. Perhaps we should put them someplace where we can both have access to them if we need them. How about in the garage?"

"That is a good idea. Mr. Steele stopped by. He said he has two horses that owners have given up. They're still in good shape. No special feeding necessary, but it's time for worming and hoof care. Here's the phone number to call if you want to take them. The owners signed a paper saying they won't expect them back. I got wormer from the feedstore and made an appointment with the ferrier for next week in case you say si."

I grinned as I looked at Gage's familiar number on the smudged piece of paper Sergio handed to me. "I'm surprised you didn't just say si for me."

He laughed. "I almost did. I'll get two stalls ready."

Later, when Gage was delivering the new horses, a gray Lincoln was following his truck and horse trailer down the lane. I wondered if it was the previous owners. It wasn't. It was Aaron Davis, the new preacher that Cindy and I had stopped to welcome to the neighborhood.

"Hello, Mr. Davis."

"Reverend Davis, if you don't mind. I haven't seen you in church. I came by to extend another sincere invitation to become a member of my congregation."

"Thank you for stopping by. Sorry I can't chat. I'm just a bit busy right now."

"Of course. Would you have dinner with me Saturday night? I'll pick you up about six."

I gawked at him. "I'm sorry. I don't know you."

"Come get to know me."

"I don't think I'm interested, but thank you for the invitation." I quickly turned away.

Sergio stood close by the trailer, holding lead shanks, willing to bring a horse from the trailer. Gage was already in the trailer. I took a lead and quietly let the horse know I was coming by, speaking and putting a hand on his rump as I squeezed in beside him and let it keep contact along his body to his head. He was calm and backed out of the trailer like a pro. We gave them time to look around, and that was when they began to snort, toss their heads, and jig.

"Let's put them in their stalls to give them time to settle," I suggested.

I didn't expect to cry over well-kept horses. Their coats were winter thick, but you could tell they were groomed regularly. Their eyes were bright with good health.

As we led them to the stall row, they danced on the end of their leads, heads high, ears pricked, neighing their anxiety. *Where are we? Where are our people? Have we been sold? Why would our people sell us? What did we do wrong?*

It obviously wasn't just abuse cases that were sad.

They were beautiful geldings. One was a buckskin called Buckshot. The other was a gray with black legs, mane, and tail named Thundercloud. We put them in side-by-side stalls. I asked Gage what sort of people the previous owners were.

"They're probably nearing retirement age. Early sixties maybe? They were boarding at Madison's until Rob lost his job. They can live on Tracy's income, but it won't support the horses. They asked that if possible, they be given to someone that will provide a good home. I immediately thought of you. I didn't tell you, and I should have, that another stipulation was that you not sell them. They asked that if you can't keep them for any reason, you'll give them to someone else who will love and appreciate them, not exploit them."

"Will you tell them they can come see them and ride them anytime they want? Just give me a call when they want to come. I would very much like to meet them."

"I'll pass that message on."

Doug called that evening. "I heard you took in Rob and Tracy's horses."

"Do you know them?"

"They were boarding at Madison's, so I've vetted them. They were good owners. They loved those horses. I really feel bad for them, and I'm glad you took them. How many stalls do you have left?"

"Four. Why? Do you have more rescue cases for me?"

"No." Doug hesitated. "Jillian, you really knock my socks off."

"Excuse me?"

He chuckled. "You're something special. I don't mean to crowd you, rush you, or scare you off, but I really want to be a part of your life even if it's just as a friend . . . although that would be hard. I'd like to board my horse at your place, and I know you don't want boarders, and maybe you don't want me around that much . . . yet."

"You have a horse?"

"Yes. I board him at Madison's right now."

"Won't she be upset if you quit boarding there?"

"No. Taz is in her staff wing until something else opens up. And she always has a waiting list."

"It would be quite a ways for you to come see him." It was almost a whisper. I didn't seem to be able to inhale.

"I'm moving up your way. We have a number of clientele in your general area, so Madison is opening another animal clinic in Clear Point. Actually, I'll be mostly working out of it."

I realized I wasn't breathing and tried to exhale slowly, quietly.

"I know I'm hitting you with an awful lot. Just promise me that, until you can get your head around it, you'll save me a stall."

I couldn't seem to get an answer to come out of my mouth.

"I'll talk to you later," said Doug. I heard the soft click as he hung up.

I had wanted to shout "Yes, yes, yes!" But all I could think was *What if it goes cold as Daniel and I had?*

CHAPTER TWENTY

Buck and Cloud ignored their food. Their stools turned to mush. They stood facing the adjoining corners of their stalls. Occasionally they'd lift a leg as if they were going to kick and then, remembering their manners, would just stamp their hoof instead. They took to laying their ears flat on their heads and snapping bared teeth at us. We lunged them for exercise, being afraid that if we turned them loose in the paddock, pasture, or arena, we'd have difficulty catching them again.

Cindy came as usual on Saturday all smiles and looking like something special had happened. I warned her to be careful around the two newcomers, and she sobered immediately. We went to the barn, and she started down the cemented aisle toward the newly filled stalls. But when Buck stretched his neck out over the stall guard with teeth showing and anger in his eyes, she stopped and stood still. I knew she was communicating with them. Buck shook his head as though denying something and pulled back into his stall. Cloud stood looking at Cindy, and even I could see the sadness in his dark eyes.

My eyes were welling with tears. Cindy turned abruptly and went to Fancy's stall. After standing awhile with her arms around her neck, she brought her out crosstied and groomed and then saddled her for a ride in the arena. I was forcing myself to not pester her with questions. I could tell she was really upset, and I very much wanted to respect her silence. I thought it must be very painful to experience what the two new geldings were going through. So I put Hobbit in the crossties for a vigorous grooming as well. As usual, I felt calmed by her presence. When Cindy and Fancy disappeared into the arena, Hobbit bumped me with her nose and whickered.

"What is it, my lovely? Want to go for a ride?"

I put a bareback pad on her back, noting how well her body was filling out. Her coat was thick and soft. I took her to the big arena where Cindy and Fancy were walking in fifteen-meter circles and figure eights. Hobbit and I warmed up at a walk, and then I tried a small nudge to her barrel. She went smoothly into a trot. I was ecstatic. Another milestone passed. After once around the arena, I slowed my mare back to a walk and gave her enough rein to stretch her neck.

Fancy trotted up alongside us. "Are you okay, Cindy?"

"I don't know. It's so hard knowing how animals are so hurt by what people do. It's sad enough listening to the abused ones, but I think it's just as bad for the ones that loved their people and were loved back and don't understand what happened."

"I know. I was thinking the same thing."

"I tried to tell them Rob and Tracy couldn't help it. I asked them to give you a chance to love them. Cloud might, but Buck is really angry. It'll take him longer. Maybe he won't be able to at all."

"Is there something I can do to help ease their pain?"

"Just love them and accept it if they can't ever really trust you."

"I will, Cindy. I'm sorry. You looked so happy when you first got here. I didn't mean to ruin your day."

"Sometimes I think I can't take any more . . . knowing. Things were just calming down."

"And then I bring in more sad cases. It must be so hard on you. You are so strong. I want you to be happy coming here, but if you can't or if you just want to be with Fancy and then leave, I understand."

"Sometimes that is what I want. But I want to help give them hope too."

"Do you want to go home after your ride?"

Cindy thought for a while. We heard tires reaching for gravel beneath the layer of snow, and soon Mindi's voice rang out. "Hello, Pip." We heard little hoofbeats and big hoof clomps on the cement aisle as Sugar and Pip were put in crossties.

Cindy gave a wan smile. "No. There's happiness here too. Look how far they've all come. They all have brand-new lives because of you."

"And you. Cindy, I'm so glad you've come into my life. You are wise beyond your years. You've been a very big part in helping these horses."

"Speaking of helping," she said, brightened, "there's a new girl at school. We're becoming friends. I don't think Nanny is getting enough attention from Milagro and Joaquin this winter. Nanny would be a good one to introduce Tatum to."

"Can you share Tatum's story with me?"

"Her mom and dad got divorced. Her dad is going to London for his job. I think her mom just doesn't want bothered, so she's living with her grandparents. Both her parents are paying child support, so she can have about anything she wants . . . except her parents. Her grandparents are really nice, and they love her to bits."

"But that doesn't ease the pain of being abandoned by her folks."

"Isn't that weird? She didn't even like it at home, but it still makes her angry."

"Maybe eventually she'll see what a stroke of luck it was to be taken in by her grandparents."

Cindy grinned. "And to get me for a friend."

"That's right."

"I think we're gonna be best friends."

"That means you need something special as a Christmas gift for your new friend."

"She really likes jewelry. She has three piercings in each ear and a belly button piercing."

"Oh dear. How about a best friend necklace?"

"I think she'd find that too childish. I'm thinking a St. Christopher necklace for protection."

I was surprised. "Oh, Cindy, I didn't know you were Catholic."

"I'm not, but Tatum is . . . kinda. And we can all use all the help we can get."

I smiled. "You're right. We do. A riding helmet would provide some protection as well."

Cindy laughed. "Yep. That too."

Sissy and Mindi led their mounts into the arena. Shouts of good morning echoed across the distance. Cindy and I left soon after, still being careful not to overdo it with riding. After we groomed our horses, we took them to the pasture without blankets. I saw that Sunset was out already. When we returned to the stall row, Cindy went to work with Nanny. Sergio had Buck in crossties. He calmly groomed, expertly avoiding snapping teeth, stamping hooves, and swishing tail. I got out grooming tools and brought Cloud out of his stall.

"Sergio, aren't you going to ride?"

"I rode early this morning. I wanted time to work with Buck."

"Do you ever sleep?"

He grinned. "Si. I checked the barn at eleven and four. I sleep in between."

"I checked at one. You're going to wear yourself out."

Cloud was standing calmly under my hands.

"Senora, Mr. Todd wants me to start welding school in the January session. There isn't much farmwork right now. It would be a good time."

"But Elena isn't done with her schooling yet. Is he in a hurry to get you through school?"

Sergio didn't answer.

"Does he have new people to find jobs for?"

Sergio kept his hands moving, his mouth silent.

"You know, Sergio, Frank has a good heart, but you don't have to let him push you around."

"That was the deal."

"Well, I didn't sign any deal with him. I hired you. I'm very pleased with your work. I don't want to lose you. And after you get your welding skills, you'll be even harder to let go. You'll be more marketable and will need a raise. I probably can't pay what a real full-time welding job will pay, but that will be your choice, not Frank Todd's."

"Gracias, Jillian."

I smiled. That was the second time he had called me Jillian. I could get used to that. "And besides, we are swamped with horse coddling and barn checks right now. You already aren't getting enough sleep. I'd say adding school to your workload is out of the question."

That night, I crawled into bed exhausted, knowing that a welding shield would be what I'd get Sergio for Christmas.

Buck and Cloud had come with their own tack and full-care equipment, including coolers, blankets, fly masks, and tack boxes full of grooming tools. Still, I was thinking of making another trip to the Double E Equine Store just to feel the quality of the different brands of merchandise I had been researching on the Internet and to purchase Cindy's Christmas gift of paddock boots.

As my eyes closed, I wondered what I'd name my store. Did I want it on the farm or in town? I needed another pasture fenced in. My stomach growled. I had forgotten to eat again.

CHAPTER TWENTY-ONE

The days slid by. For several days, it snowed huge airy flakes. Sergio plowed them into large piles on which Milagro, Joaquin, and Duchess played "king of the mountain." Then the temperatures dropped, and we all took to staying in as much as we could. Sergio and I set up a barn-check routine. If he got up twice during the night, I did the morning chores. If it was my turn for the night checks, he did the morning chores. We changed the check times each night. It seemed the visitors weren't going to return.

Sissy reminded me that I was expected for Christmas dinner, so I invited Doug for a Christmas Eve dinner. I was done with my shopping. I had two weeks to finish wrapping.

Over the next few days, the geldings began to eat better, and their stools returned to normal. Cloud was trying to accept the situation and move on. Buck's ground manners improved, but he was still sullen. Tracy Poindexter called to thank me for taking their horses. I tried to coax her into coming out for a ride, but they thought it would be too painful.

"Why don't you try to see it as I'm just taking care of them until you get back on your feet?"

"We signed that paper."

I knew what paper. It was in my file drawer, but I answered, "I didn't see any paper."

"And we've already lost our stalls at Phoenix."

"You can board here when you're ready."

"Rob isn't having much luck finding a job at his age."

"Then they have a home here. It would be a help if you came to help care for and exercise them."

"I just don't know. That's a good distance to travel."

"I do understand that. If you ever want to, please feel free to come visit them."

"Thank you again for taking them. Gage and Doug both speak highly of you. Have a merry Christmas."

"You too."

I thought her tone sounded like the topic was closed, and I was ashamed that I was relieved that I wasn't going to have boarders. But the more horses we had, the harder it was to give them all adequate attention. It got a bit dull grooming so many. I decided to make things more interesting by starting bombproof training with flags, fans, bright flashing lights, loud noises, and unfamiliar surfaces. I would go to the Goodwill to get an old mattress, pick up some tarps at the hardware store, and get Sergio to make a broad teeter-totter. It would be almost like training Duchess for agility. It was going to be fun.

By the next day, we had the tarps scattered about the arena. Some had the shiny side up, and others had the colored side up. There were two mattresses. I started just leading the horses across the strange surfaces. Hobbit stopped to look at and smell everything. It took a bit of encouragement, but she finally danced across them as if on tiptoe. Sergio was right there with Sunset to be part of the excitement.

When I tried leading the other mares across the obstacles, I found out just how much Hobbit must trust me. They were all much more reluctant to be cooperative. All the horses seemed disturbed by the sound of the tarps as much as by the sight of them.

Cindy was really excited about the new training. Even Mindi worked on leading Pip over the tarps and mattresses. Sissy was nervous about working with Sugar.

"You must walk across them as if it's no threat, Sissy. Don't stop to look back at Sugar. Just walk ahead confidently like you expect her to follow. If she dances around it, just keep moving forward to the next. If she succeeds, be sure to praise her."

Once the horses could handle being led across the strange surfaces, we started riding them across. Within a week, we added a radio and started playing it softly. We hung a banner from a shepherd's hook. We hung one from the ceiling that could be raised and lowered to get the horses used to going under it or by it, letting it brush against them. I had big plans for having several dangling. Then we would add fans to make them flutter and wave. We would have the steadiest horses in the area by the time we were done.

Doug showed up on Saturday while we were riding the horses around, past, and over the obstacles.

"That looks like fun," he called across the arena.

"Grab a horse and join us," I called back.

"Make a difference which one?"

"Why don't you work with Buck? I think he'll need a stronger hand. I'll warn you we haven't had him in here yet. We've been mostly working with the mares and Sunset."

It turned out Buck dealt with the obstacles best of all the horses. While the others sniffed the tarps as they crossed them, grabbed at the banners with their teeth, and almost danced in time with whatever song was playing on the radio, Buck walked calmly over, around, and through it all.

"We're going to have to find something more challenging for him, I think," said Doug, sitting easy in the Western saddle.

"It appears so," I replied. "Maybe moving obstacles like a teeter-totter and that huge ball to push his chest against. That might help him get his mind off his loss."

Doug looked at Cindy. "What do you think, Cindy?"

"I think Jillian is right. Mr. Poindexter used him for trail riding. Buck was pretty bored with it."

"So we need to find him a job where he can show off his abilities and be challenged," I said thoughtfully.

"He'd make a good police horse," suggested Doug as he and Buck drew close to Hobbit and me.

"Is there a search-and-rescue team in this area?" I questioned to no one in particular.

Sissy answered, "No, but there is an ancillary crowd control group that helps at fairs, parades, and outdoor concerts at the park."

I could feel excitement tug at the corners of my lips.

"Doug, are you busy this evening?"

"No."

"Care to come for dinner?"

"By all means, yes."

Everyone was busy putting their horses back in their stalls, and then suddenly, it was just Doug and me with Cloud and Nanny in the arena. We worked in silence for a while, and then I asked Doug when the new clinic would be opening.

"We've got a location. It's a matter of getting the equipment in and hiring another vet. I've found an apartment that will be available the first of February."

"Will you wait until then to bring your horse?"

"I'd rather bring him as soon as possible to take advantage of the new curriculum."

I grinned at him. "Anytime."

Cindy and Sergio were scrubbing the last of the feed pans and water buckets. We put the top three hierarchy mares in the arena so we could muck their stalls, and we were thinking that they'd get even more used to the obstacles that way. Then we switched the first group out for Hobbit, Sunset, and Pip while we cleaned those stalls. Buck and Cloud were last. When all the horses were on clean bedding, I said to no one and everyone, "How about some Scrabble?"

I had broiled steaks, broccoli and cheese over baked potatoes, and a fruit salad for dinner. It was nearing dusk, and Doug was saying he could drop Cindy off at her home when the doorbell rang. Duchess gave one loud woof and looked at me to ask if I needed any more encouragement to attend to the matter.

It was snowing again. A new two inches covered the ground. At the door stood a grizzled man in an army peacoat, jeans, work boots, and a cap with earflaps he was in the process of folding up. Next to him stood a child with Down syndrome who was clinging to the edge of the man's coat pocket with a mittened hand, although he looked like he could be a teenager.

"Hi. I'm Jeffrey Rawling, and this is my son, JC."

The boy looked up at his dad at the sound of his name.

"Hello, JC," I said cheerfully.

He hid his face in his father's side.

"He's kind of shy."

"What can I do for you, Jeffrey?"

"Sometimes when we pass your place, your horses are out and JC gets so excited. I was wondering if he could pet them."

There was emptiness in his blue eyes; there was no expression on his face. He wasn't meeting my eyes.

"Sure. Let me get my coat." As I turned away, I saw a flash of surprise cross the man's face, and a big O appeared where JC's mouth had been as he looked up at his father. The man and boy turned toward the barn. Doug was behind me with his coat on, holding mine so I could slip my arms in. Cindy and Duchess followed us out and dashed ahead to open the stall row's sliding door.

Doug nudged my arm and pointed down. I immediately saw what he saw: the prints of big boots and smaller boots.

Sergio appeared at our side, ready to be of assistance. Cindy had all the stall doors slid back. The horses stood at the stall guards, curious about what was happening. Nanny stretched her neck toward JC, straining against the stall guard. JC walked right up to her, leaned his forehead against hers, and put his hands on either side of her muzzle. After a moment, she wiggled her lips on his cheek as if looking for a choice blade of grass. JC giggled and kissed her nose.

I could tell he wanted to stay with her, but he also wanted to meet the others. When he got to Pip, he patted him on his back, called him a big dog, and let out a big *woof, woof.* Duchess cocked her head at JC, and Pip whinnied. Then JC tried to whinny. Even Hobbit came to greet JC. She put her nose in the crook of JC's neck and blew. JC hunched his shoulders and laughed. He patted Sunset and said, "Pretty horse." Buck wasn't at his stall door, so JC passed it and went to Cloud. With his eyes on the big gray, he asked "Ride?" as though Cloud would be the one to answer.

Jeffrey had stopped at Buck's stall to gaze at the big buckskin. With some trepidation, I watched him unhook the stall guard, enter the stall, and hook the guard behind him. He laid his hand on Buck's back and just stood there.

Sergio went to the tack room and came back. As Jeffrey turned to ask if he could groom the horse., Sergio handed him a brush before the words could leave his mouth. Then he snapped a lead onto Cloud's halter, slipped the halter over the gray's head, and led him out of the stall. He took JC by the hand and led them both to the arena.

We all followed. I was nervous about leaving Jeffrey alone with Buck within the confines of a stall. And I was thinking things were moving a bit too fast with JC and Cloud. But I seemed to be swept along in the momentum.

Doug made a stirrup by lacing his fingers. I showed JC how to put his foot in it and swing his leg over Cloud's back. I heard JC's quick intake of breath and saw his worried expression as he realized how high he was, but Doug showed him how to grasp a handful of mane. Then keeping a hand on JC's leg and speaking to him softly, he walked alongside them as Sergio led Cloud around the arena.

When we returned Cloud to his stall, Jeffrey had Buck in the crossties, and Cindy was showing him how to pick a hoof. JC tugged on his father's coat. "Dad. Again?"

"I don't know, JC."

"Of course, you can come again. Thursday about four o'clock would work for us."

JC smiled up at his father, and his father looked at me, his eyes and mouth both saying thank you.

"I'm jealous," whispered Doug as we watched father and son leave.

"Well, if you aren't working, you can come too."

He planted a quick kiss on my cheek. "Thanks." He smiled as he climbed into his truck to take Cindy home.

Sergio and I decided we could discontinue the nighttime barn checks.

CHAPTER TWENTY-TWO

On Thursday just after noon, Doug called to ask if it would be a good day to bring Taz to the barn since he was coming anyway.

"Sure. I'll have a stall ready for him."

"Could I bring him now?"

"Well, I really need to study for semifinals."

"I won't bother you. I thought I'd ride and start introducing him to the bombproof course. And I'd like to stay to make you dinner."

"That sounds wonderful. See you in a bit."

I called Sergio to have him get the stall ready. I got my study materials assembled at the desk in my bedroom. It was cold outside, and I wanted Doug to be free to come inside after he worked with Raz Ama Taz without interrupting my study time. I hit the books for an hour until I heard Doug pull in. I decided a break was in order so I could go meet Taz. Doug was just backing his horse out of the trailer as I bolted from the house. Taz stood over sixteen hands. He was a liver chestnut with a stripe on his face, a white sock on his left front leg, and a white stocking on his right rear leg. He was well muscled.

"Wow. He's beautiful."

"Thanks. I thought you were studying?"

"I was and will again, but I wanted to come meet him."

"Jillian, meet Raz Ama Taz. Taz, this is Jillian, that very special lady I was telling you about."

I could feel my face getting hot. "Quarter horse?" I questioned, trying to hide my embarrassment.

"Yes. You know your breeds."

"You look well matched. How do you keep him so muscled?"

"A lot of ride time."

"I thought so. But how do you work it in with the hours you work?"

"Well, before I met you, I had a lot of time on my hands. But no matter how tired I am, he needs at least a half hour of exercise six days a week—preferably more, but at least that much to keep him calm and happy."

"Well, enjoy. I'm going back to study. Feel free to come in whenever you're done with Taz. You know where everything is."

When I heard Doug working in the kitchen, I looked at the clock. It was four thirty. The daylight was fading. I needed to switch on a light or end my study time. I went to the window and stared out. For some reason, I didn't want to go downstairs. I sat in the chair near the window and watched the falling snowflakes turn from dark specks against a pale sky to light specks against a dark sky. Wonderful aromas began wafting into my room, and I let my nose follow the scents down to the kitchen, with Duchess clambering down the stairs in front of me. She trotted into the kitchen, where Doug roughed her just behind the ears and jowls.

"Hey there, Duchess." He looked up at me. "Are you all right?"

"Yes, why?"

"I guess I thought you wanted to be in the barn when Jeff and JC were here."

I slapped my forehead. "Oh gosh, I forgot."

"I didn't want to bother you if you were studying. Sergio took care of them. They wanted to come back again, so he said next Thursday at four again. Is that okay?"

"That'll work. Sergio is so dependable."

"You also had another visitor, but I sent him packing."

"And that was . . . ?"

"Reverend Davis."

"Thank you." I grinned.

"You're welcome." He grinned back. "My pleasure."

I looked at him quizzically.

"Less competition," he clarified.

"Gosh, it smells good. When did you learn to cook?"

"I got tired of opening boxes and cans, so I took a cooking class many years ago soon after my lady friend told me she couldn't wait any longer."

"How long before chow time?"

"Fifteen minutes."

"I'm gonna run down and help with the feeding."

Once I was out in the cold air, I chided myself. What *was* my problem? I kept swinging from wanting to be with Doug to wanting to get away from him. I acknowledged it as fear, and I was doing a poor job of loving as if I'd never been hurt. I couldn't even really say I'd been hurt as I had been the inflexible one.

As I was returning to the house, the snowy owl swooped right in front of me so fast I instinctively dodged. When I looked around for it, it was nowhere to be seen. She wasn't perched on the garage peak or on the wing in the sky. *What is with that owl?* I wondered.

Shedding my coat, I asked Doug, "Did you see that owl dive-bomb me?"

"I saw you duck, but I didn't see anything that would cause you to dip like that. I thought maybe you slipped on a slick spot."

He was putting bowls of food on the table.

"Let me wash my hands quick." I dashed to the half bath, and as I lathered my hands, I thought, *Darn. Now I have to wonder if I'm losing my mind.*

Over dinner, Doug got me talking about the equine supply store I was considering. He thought opening it at the farm would be best until business picked up. I suggested he keep an eye open for someone to man it for me.

"What about Cindy? Just after school for a couple hours. She could do her homework if it wasn't busy. During the day, you could have a sign to 'Honk your horn for store attendant.'"

"That's worth considering. I'm not wanting a lot of business. I just want to provide more of a selection than what the feedstore has and so I don't have to drive the two hours to and from the Double E."

"You might be surprised at the business volume you get. I've heard a lot of comments about that very problem. I really think there's a market for it. And I'm sure Madison will let you put a flyer up at all her farms."

"One problem, however. I don't think Cindy wants to be here as much. All these troubled horses weigh on her, and she has a new friend at school that might be occupying more of her time."

"Well, you can keep it in mind. You never know how things will turn out."

"And I need to get a building erected."

"I have a contractor friend that can help with that."

"Great."

"Gage is a licensed electrician, so he can help with that. I'm handy with a hammer and nail. I'm sure Sergio could help. So between the four of us, I'll bet we could put up a mighty fine building for you."

"That would be super, but Sergio might be in welding school, so his time will be limited."

"How is he going to keep up with sowing, harvesting, and all the maintenance work around here if he's in school?"

"I'm worried about that too. I might have to hire some part-time help, but I've got a few months to worry about that."

As Doug left later, he pressed a check into my hand. "It's the same as Madison charges, but if it isn't enough, let me know. I know you didn't really want boarders."

"I feel bad taking it."

"That was the deal, so you have to." He smiled. "I'm just grateful you let Taz in so he'll be closer to where I'll actually be."

By the next week, temperatures had warmed up into the lower thirties; and the sun made a regular appearance each day, melting the snow inch by inch. Sissy and Mindi came every day about one o'clock after a half day of preschool. By then, I had helped feed, mucked stalls, ridden, lunged horses and was working on my inside routine. Twice a week, Sissy got a riding lesson so as to not overtax Sugar. One day, Sissy knocked on the door.

"Hi, Sissy. What can I do for you?"

"It's more like what can I do for you? We're coming so often. Can I pay you or help you in some way?"

"Well, come in for some coffee and cookies and milk." I smiled down at Mindi. "And let's talk."

Once we were settled, I continued, "You're already helping by giving Pip and Sugar TLC. I do have some projects for this summer that you might be able to help with."

I told her about the store and fencing in a new pasture. She volunteered her husband, Dylan, for the manual labor but offered to man the store a few hours a couple of times a week. I assured her we could set down specifics closer to warmer weather. She reminded me about Christmas dinner before she left.

On Thursday, I remembered that Jeffrey and JC were coming. At three forty-five, I headed for the barn. Doug was pulling in.

"Hey there, good-looking." I immediately blushed at my boldness. He beamed. I scrambled for something else to say to cover my embarrassment. "About time you showed up. Taz might start missing you."

"I've been here every day since I brought him."

"Oh. I didn't realize that."

"I'm not going to bug you. I don't want you to get tired of me and boot me out."

I didn't need to reply as Jeffrey pulled in. JC bolted out the back door and yanked open the front door of the sedan. Jeffrey, in the meantime, had approached me.

"Jillian, I'm sorry if I've overstepped my bounds, but my mother wanted to come. Is that all right?"

"Sure," I said too quickly. Then I saw the elderly woman leaning heavily on JC. Jeffrey went to get a walker out of the trunk, and I scurried into the stall row to slide back the stall doors. Sergio was already there. The stall doors were open, the horses at the guards were watching the activity, there were grooming supplies by Buck's stall, and Cloud was in the crossties being groomed by Sergio.

I heard the old lady's quick intake of breath as she saw all the equine heads overhanging stall guards and peering in her direction. Naturally, as Nanny was in the first stall, it was Nanny she went to and seemed to stick to. She looked down the aisle at the others. Maybe she didn't think she could go any farther. But she stood grasping Nanny's mane as though to hold herself up. She leaned against the horse's chest and rested her head against the horse's neck, closed her eyes, and smiled. Her body seemed to melt into a relaxed stance.

Jeffrey had Buck in the crossties and was placidly grooming, his mouth moving in words only the horse could hear. Buck's ears twitched to catch every word. JC, with a big grin on his face, was confidently grooming Cloud under Sergio's tutelage.

"Look at that," I whispered, leaning back into Doug's chest. "It's almost as if the horses cast a magic spell over everyone."

"Yes, it does," Doug agreed softly.

"Mrs. Rawling, would you like to sit down?"

"I would, but I want to stay with the horse too."

"Didn't I see a lawn chair in the tack room?" asked Doug.

"You did. If you get it for us, I'll get Mrs. Rawling into the arena so she can sit to watch JC ride. Then we can bring Nanny in to be close to Mrs. Rawling. Jeffrey, are you going to ride?"

"I don't know how. I wouldn't mind some lessons sometime, but for now, I'll just groom." Buck stood with eyes half closed in pleasure as the gentle hands brushed away dust, tension, and mistrust.

After the old woman was seated, I positioned Nanny behind her. She cooperated by hanging her head over Mrs. Rawling's shoulder. I got myself a chair from the observation area and sat next to her.

"Aren't they beautiful? I've always loved horses," related the wrinkled Mrs. Rawling.

"Did you have one?"

"No. My parents couldn't afford one. Then my husband insisted they were dangerous and a needless expense. Oh, you have no idea what a joy it is to sit here petting and watching my boys enjoy them as well. Thank you for helping my boys."

"I haven't really done much."

"You've given them hope."

"I've just given them some horse time."

"But the difference in them is magical."

My heart jumped at the similar observation to what I had just made to Doug.

"Jeffrey just got back from Iraq a few months ago. While he was over there, his wife left him and JC. I've been trying to care for JC, but I'm feeling my age. I was so worried about them. Jeffrey hasn't been able to find work, and he was taking his anger and despair out on JC. But he's calmer now; he has more patience with JC. He's looking for a job again and went down to the college to check on classes. You'll continue to help them, won't you?"

Her eyes were closed as she stroked Nanny's face. I wondered if she was talking to me or to Nanny.

CHAPTER TWENTY-THREE

It was the day before Christmas. The low temperatures of the previous week had held, and the snow had started falling early. By the time we went to the barn to feed, there were four inches on the ground. Car tracks made dark scars through the white flesh. We all groomed our horses as they ate their evening meal. We saved the treats for after. Mindi had brought carrots, Sergio had apples, and Cindy revealed peppermint candies.

With all of us in the arena, it was chaos at first. I suggested formation riding. We formed a column. Doug on Taz and I on Hobbit led side by side. Sergio on Sunset and Cindy on Fancy came next, with Joaquin on Cloud and Milagro on Nanny following. Sissy on Sugar and Mindi on Pip brought up the rear. We rode down the middle of the arena and then separated, going down opposite sides, meeting and reuniting the column at the other end. We trotted down the middle then broke apart to do a twenty-meter circle in opposite directions before continuing down the center. Everyone laughed as Mindi and Pip skipped the circling part. As we got to the end, we went to opposite corners and then went diagonally across the arena to the opposite corner, trying to alternate horses through the center, laughing as two horses got through at once or almost collided. The leaders then took the rear positions to give others a chance to lead the drill. The horses had definitely earned their treats.

When we left the barn, Doug scooped up a snowball. He hadn't even thrown it at me before six other snowballs were flying through the air, with Duchess leaping for them, catching some in her mouth. When that was over, the snowmen were being rolled and formed—walnuts for eyes, carrots for noses, red-colored popcorn for lips, and purple grapes for buttons.

At last happily exhausted, we all separated to go home to dry out and warm up. Doug took Cindy home. I took that opportunity to take a quick hot shower and put on dry clothes. When Doug got back, I suggested he hunker in front of the lit fireplace to dry out or open his Christmas gift. He opened his gift, which was a pair of his preferred brand of jeans and a flannel shirt. He quickly donned the dry clothes. We played Scrabble until the ham was done. He helped mash the potatoes while I made the vegetable, browned the rolls, and set the table in silence.

"Sounds like neither of us is a very good conversationalist," I quipped.

"Well, we've both lived alone for a long time. I'm comfortable with silence. I think it says a lot for our relationship that we can work as a team without needing a lot of babble."

I thought for a second with a smile on my lips. "Yes, I like that observation."

"Do you believe in reincarnation?"

"Yes."

"I was just wondering if we were mated way back before verbal language was necessary or safe; back when it was telepathy, body language, and hand signs."

"That's a deep thought. Do you actually think we've been coupled during any other life cycle?"

"Yes, because of the powerful feeling I had when I first met you. It was like, 'There you are. I've been waiting for you.'"

I couldn't raise my eyes to meet his. My heart was pounding. I thought surely he could hear it. He put the potatoes on the table next to the green beans. I got out the coleslaw and pie from the refrigerator.

"Shall we eat?"

It was later when we were standing side by side, me washing dishes and him drying them, that I asked, "Are you in a hurry to get home?"

"Nope."

"Do me a favor?"

"Yes."

"Don't you want to hear it first?"

"Sure, but the answer will be yes."

"I want to throw some apples up on the apartment roof while I ring some sleigh bells."

He grinned widely. "That's a definite yes."

He took the red velvet Santa's bag full of clothes, books, games, and toys up to the stair landing just outside the door and came back down, stepping backward in his own footprints so it looked like someone went up but didn't come back down. I took small bites out of the apples, which Doug then threw to bounce on the roof. I jangled the bells. He yelled, "Ho ho ho!" I jangled some more. He threw more apples and yelled, "On Dasher, on Donner and Blitzen!" More bells jangled as we hid against the garage wall, listening, waiting to be sure someone looking out the windows would not see us.

"One more favor?"

"This one will cost you," he whispered as he leaned down to softly kiss my cold lips. "What is it?"

I was embarrassed that I had to gasp for breath before I could speak. "Drop Cindy's Santa bag off at her place on your way home."

"Only if I get to ring the bells and make reindeer noises on her roof."

"I don't think she believes in Santa Claus."

"She will after tonight."

I had invited Sergio, Elena, and the kids for Christmas breakfast. When I went into the great room to turn on the Christmas lights, I saw two Christmas presents with my name on them. One wrapped in silver was from Doug. The other wrapped in red was from Cindy. *How had they gotten them in here without me knowing?* I wondered. I tore at the wrapping. Doug's gift was a pewter figurine of a woman standing next to a horse, one hand holding the lead, the other on the horse's back. I took it to my bedroom and put it on my bedside stand. Cindy's was horse-head bookends. I put them on my desk. Later, I would choose my favorite horse novels to put between them.

I heard a knock at the door. Duchess gave a bark, and we both scurried down the stairs. "Merry Christmas."

"Feliz Navidad," they chorused back.

I was pleased to see the kids wearing some of the new clothes Santa had gotten them. They jabbered on with wide eyes about sleigh bells and hearing reindeer and Santa on the roof.

"Well, shall we open some gifts before breakfast?"

Milagro squealed in delight as she clapped her hands and jumped up and down. Joaquin tried to act more dignified by biting the inside of his cheek to keep from smiling. I had gotten them each a riding helmet. They tried to hide their disappointment by saying thank you. I gave Sergio his welding helmet and Elena a stethoscope and blood pressure cuff. I knew they would be hard-pressed to provide them for themselves to start their new careers. Then from behind the tree, I found more packages for each of the kids. Milagro's was the kaleidoscope and a baby doll that drank from a bottle and immediately wet itself. Luckily, it came with a dozen diapers. Joaquin got the puzzle and a new car transport truck complete with seven cars on the trailer. There was no need to hide disappointment with those gifts.

"Now how about some blueberry pancakes?"

After we were all done eating, Elena started to clear the table.

"That's not necessary, Elena."

"It's the least I can do. Consider it my Christmas gift to you."

"Well, okay. I'll go help with the chores."

"No need," piped in Sergio with a grin. "It's already done. I just need to know if you want them put out to pasture. It's pretty cold out right now, and it's supposed to get even colder this afternoon."

"Let's put them in the arena for a couple hours to stretch their legs."

"No, senora. Joaquin and I will do it. You are going away. It is our gift to you."

"Thanks to all of you, but don't you have friends to visit?"

"Si. We will go this evening. We will put the horses back in their stalls and do evening chores."

Late that night, satiated and tired, I was heading for the back door to give Duchess a last chance to relieve herself before I went to bed. I was thinking what a grand Christmas it had been when I heard the familiar thud. Duchess and I both darted out the door and ran around the side of the house. There was no trace of the owl. We came back and went around the other side. The moon was bright, and the security light on the garage also lit that side of the house. I found a small dark feather but no owl. Instead, as goose bumps formed on my arms, I stared at the small prints of bare feet leaving a trail toward the stairs to the apartment above the garage.

My dreams that night were full of owls dive-bombing me, flying low over the earth, and leaving human footprints beneath their flight path and of black eyes watching my every move. Duchess's cold nose woke me. My arms were crossed in front of my face as though fending off an attacker. My mouth was dry.

I went to the bathroom for a drink of water. I sat at my desk to write out my thank-you notes to Doug, Cindy, Sergio, and Elena, stumbled back to bed, and woke up feeling tired and restless.

Sergio joined me as I passed the garage, heading for the barn. His eyes were bloodshot, his face slack. We both stopped and looked at each other and both burst out laughing.

"Rough night?" I asked.

"Si. And you?"

"Si."

Jeffrey called at about noon. I was having a hot tea and watching a documentary show on TV.

"I'm sorry to bother you, Jillian, but could we come out today?"

"Sure."

"Any chance you could give me some riding instructions? I think I'm ready."

"Okay, but maybe we should put you on one of the mares. Buck can be a handful."

"Could we let him decide? If he bucks me off, I'll gladly switch to another."

"That's fine. We can give it a try. Is your mom coming?"

"Is that okay? She really likes being around the horses."

"No problem."

I got into my coveralls. I wanted to lunge Fancy, Cloud, and Buck to expend some of their energy. I wanted to give Mrs. Rawling a chance to pet a different horse, and since Cindy hadn't been coming as often, I felt Fancy might like some attention.

The phone rang as I was putting on my boots. "Hello?"

"Jillian, this is Gage. How was your Christmas?"

"Wonderful. Yours?"

"Couldn't be better. I proposed to Madison, and she said yes."

"Congratulations. When's the big day?"

"Next fall. We haven't chosen a specific day yet."

"I'd better get an invite."

"You will. But the reason I called is, I have another surrendered horse. Nothing wrong with him. Thought I'd give you first crack at him."

"Gage, I've only got a few stalls left. I'd rather save them for cases no one else wants."

"Okay. But I'll probably still always call you first, and you can pick and choose which you want."

"That's a deal."

Sergio was riding Sunset in the arena as I was bringing in Fancy to lunge.

"Do you want any of the others?" he called.

"Sergio, finish your ride. Jeffrey and JC are coming. I'm just getting ready."

I got the other horses lunged and the lawn chair from the tack room waiting in the arena.

We had Mrs. Rawling in her chair with a lap robe over her shoulders and one over her legs. Fancy stood in front of her, but her large liquid eyes were on the other horses. For a moment, I thought

I had made a mistake, but Fancy stood still as the old woman leaned forward and stretched up to stroke the horse's shoulder. Fancy finally lowered her head closer to the woman so she could stroke her neck and face. I let out a sigh of relief.

Sergio was leading Cloud, with JC astride, around the arena. Jeffrey sat on Buck, listening intently as I was explaining the ear, shoulder, hip, and heel alignment.

"And when you cue your horse, as soon as he starts to do it, quit cuing."

"What do you mean?"

"Let's say you want him to walk forward. Squeeze your calves against his sides only as long as it takes for him to respond. His reward is you quit squeezing him. If he needs more than a squeeze, maybe you need to give a soft kick with your heels, or a hard kick. But as soon as he responds, quit kicking. Same with when you want him to stop. Try just squeezing the reins in your hands. If he stops, release the squeeze. If he doesn't stop, pull back a little, or more and more until he does. But when he does, immediately release the pressure. You want to cue as little as it takes to get the desired results."

"Okay."

"Now pick up the reins but keep your hands just above his withers."

"What's that?"

"That bump right at the bottom of his neck. Good. Now what do you feel at the other end?"

He thought a moment. "Is that a trick question? At the other end of the horse?"

"No. The other end of the reins."

"I don't really feel anything."

I chuckled. "Okay, slowly shorten your reins until you make contact with the bit and go no further. You don't want to be pulling on it. You just want to make contact."

As Jeffrey began to shorten the reins, Buck's ears began to twitch and his head came up slightly. Jeffrey smiled. "I got it."

"Did you notice Buck's ears twitch and his head come up when you made contact?"

"Yes."

"The reins are your telegraph line to Buck. You want to be as easy on his mouth as possible. You want to maintain contact without yanking on him. So when he walks and his head bobs a little, make sure your grip on the reins is soft enough to go forward and backward to maintain that contact without pulling or yanking.

"Now when you want to go around a curve, you'll just squeeze the rein of the direction you want to turn. If he doesn't curve, pull slightly and let up as soon as he starts to go into the curve. You need to look in the direction you want him to go as your weight shift will also signal him to go in that direction. You don't want him to turn his head. He should just curve at the poll, which is here." I touched the top of Buck's head just behind his ears. "If it's a sharp turn, I use my heel to touch his side as far back as I can reach on the side I want him to turn towards. That cues him to realign his hips as he curves his body so that his whole body is then headed in the new direction. And remember to look in the new direction as well. Are you ready?"

"I'm not sure."

"I'll walk along with you. Oh, one more thing. Sit relaxed, and let your pelvis move with the horse. It'll feel like your pelvis is disconnected from the rest of your body. You don't want your legs bumping against his sides unless you are cuing him. So put just enough weight in the stirrups to keep them still. So go ahead and squeeze both of your calves."

Buck stepped out nicely. There was no way I could keep up with his long stride, so I moved into the center of the ring where my circle would be smaller than his. Jeffrey was doing well. I could tell he was trying to remember everything.

"Now don't pull on the reins, but squeeze them and stop letting your pelvis move."

Buck stopped. I saw Jeffrey's hands release his squeeze on the reins.

"Not bad. Try to release a bit sooner. As soon as you feel him, stop. Go forward again."

I let them make a lap around the arena before I asked for another stop. "Good. Pat him, and tell him he's a good boy. Now go ahead and practice that much. Try to get a feel for what his body is doing under you. You want to feel him pushing forward from his hindquarters, not pull forward with the front quarters."

I went to sit with Mrs. Rawling. She looked tired. "How are you, Mrs. Rawling?"

"Call me Emma, please."

"I'm glad you came along, Emma."

"Thank you for letting me. I've so enjoyed being this close to the horses. I cried last night because it didn't happen until the end of my life."

"Well, you be sure to come every time Jeffrey and JC come, and we'll make up for lost time."

"Thank you, Jillian. You are so kind."

"I have to go away in a bit, but Sergio will take care of you. Do you think you'll be okay sitting here?'

"Oh, yes. JC made me bring the lap rugs. He's such a special child. I don't understand how Peggy could leave him behind."

"I'll bet she regrets it one day. You take care, Emma. I'll see you Thursday."

She just smiled and leaned her cheek against Fancy's jowl.

CHAPTER TWENTY-FOUR

As long as the wind wasn't blowing and the temperatures held at about thirty degrees, the horses went to pasture without blankets. We were getting days of fluffy large snow floating from the sky to fill the sled and boot tracks. Each morning, the ground started pristine, but it didn't last long. It was good to hear the children's laughter again as they played, churning up the new snow. Duchess always wanted to go out when she heard their voices.

Joaquin and Milagro had returned to school, but I was still on break. I had no studying to do, so I went on the Internet to look up shape-shifters. I wasn't satisfied with the information that was mostly about the modern version of them. I was sure I had read that the pre-Columbian Indians were able to shape-shift, converse with animals, and even understand the wind's messages. But there was only a small paragraph on shape–shifting, and it limited it to shamans shifting into their totem animals. I went to the library, but they had nothing on the topic either.

Even if only shamans could do it, I did believe Wee Shee qualified at least as a healer. I remembered well the bitter brew that eliminated the pain I had struggled with last spring. I wondered if there was a lesson or a message in her shape-shifting. Was it that I could be anything I wanted, even something different from what I was? Or was it maybe that I could choose how I saw things and others? I thought it would be nice to fly above my mundane feelings or those of fear—fear of going back to the isolation I was in just last spring. I wanted to embrace Doug without worrying about losing him and without fearing that the pain that would follow that rejection would be too much to bear.

I thought of the evening that he made me dinner. He hadn't seen the owl dive-bomb me, but he was watching out the window for my return. He had already told me he thought we were soul mates and that even if I couldn't accept him as a lover, he still wanted to be my friend. How long could he stand waiting for me not to turn tail and run every time I had doubts?

One evening, I bundled up and took a lap rug out to sit on a bench. I put the lap rug down to sit on to diminish the cold. It was dark; clouds hid the stars. The snow came down, making tiny tick sounds as it landed on bare branches and the dry, plumy long stems of the spent pampas grass. Duchess rolled, her big body crunching through the frozen old crust of previous snows. She ran, her huge paws punching holes in the top layer, kicking up the softer snow beneath. She buried her face in it and snapped at the airborne snow, going up or coming down, with her mouth. I had to smile at her exuberance.

I heard a vehicle. Frank Todd's pickup parked in front of the garage. I saw him go around the corner. I assumed he went up the stairs to the apartment. It was too cold to stay out long, so I was at the kitchen window when Frank left a half hour later. Soon after, I saw Sergio go to the barn. The lights in the stall row came on, followed by the arena lights. I knew he was riding Sunset, apparently using his horse to calm himself as I did with Hobbit.

I went upstairs, lit candles in the bathroom, and ran hot water for a soak. As I sank down into the bubbles and felt my muscles relax, my mind wandered over the past seven months. It had been a whirlwind of activity. People and horses had flooded into my life. The harvesting had been hectic. I wasn't sure I wanted so much activity in my life this next year. But I didn't want to block out goodness from my life either. I didn't want to be rigid. I wanted to be able to flow through experiences to enjoy them or learn and grow from the harsher ones. I really needed to pay more attention to what was going on around me and to take time to savor what was happening, not just rush through it.

When I got out of the tub, I took a moment to relish the warmth of my prewarmed towel, robe, and slippers; the comfort of the chair; and the feel and smell of the book I was going to read. I stared out the window and saw it was snowing heavier, larger flakes.

By the time I got to the barn the next morning, it appeared that we had an additional foot of snow over the top of the foot we had previously. The lane and parking area had been plowed clear, and Sergio was grooming Sunset.

"Goodness, do you ever sleep?"

"Si, I sleep."

"Did you ride last night?"

"Si, I ride."

"I saw Frank visit you last night. It isn't any of my business, but is he nagging you about starting school?"

"Si. He's nagging."

"We've discussed this before, Sergio. With so many horses and all the snow we've been having, I just don't think I can spare you right now."

"I told him I'd go sign up."

"Well, I'll call him and tell him I can't spare you right now. The deal was for Elena to finish her schooling and get a job first. And as I said before, I hired you, not Frank."

He was smiling. "Thank you, senora."

"You're welcome. Now let's get these horses fed."

The temperatures were supposed to reach thirty-five degrees, but we decided the snow was too deep to put the horses to pasture. Pip would be almost totally hidden if we got much more snow, and it was still coming down. I rode Hobbit instead of lunging her for exercise. I spaced out some poles to start going over. Sergio rode Fancy, starting her over the poles as well. Sergio rode Buck and Cloud. I lunged the other mares and Pip. I wasn't sure if the snow would keep my regulars home or if everyone would show up to ride. But just in case, we set up the training obstacles.

I was still practicing being aware, so I looked each horse in the eye, inhaled their scent, felt their muscles and body heat, breathed deeply the aroma of hay, felt the heaviness of the mattresses and the stiffness of the tarps, noticed the pewter sky, watched Duchess trot ahead of me, and heard the tractor rumble to life as Sergio prepared to plow again.

I had just shed my coveralls when the phone rang. "Hello?"

"Jillian, this is Jeffrey."

"What can I do for you, Jeffrey?"

"Mom died last Thursday night."

I gasped. "But you were here Thursday."

"I know. She died in her sleep that night. She was buried Sunday."

"Jeffrey, I'm so sorry. I don't read the obituaries. I'd have been there if I had known."

"I don't think I can do this."

I wasn't sure what he meant by "this."

"Jeffrey, remember how much she loved the horses. I know JC does also, and I think you have a connection with Buck. I don't think Emma would want you to quit coming. In fact, I heard her ask one of the horses to watch out for you and JC."

"I don't think I can take care of JC."

"JC loves you. Just focus on one thing at a time."

There was silence.

"Please come, Jeffrey. You can do it."

No matter what I did, my mind kept worrying about Jeffrey. Had he gotten JC ready for school on time? As I swam, I heard the radio say JC's school would be cancelled the following day also. How could Jeffrey look for a job or go to his classes if JC was still at home? As I made a salad for lunch, I wondered about Jeffrey's cooking skills. I decided to invite them for dinner if they showed up that evening. I got out a roast and put it in the Crock-Pot. I washed potatoes and scrubbed carrots to add to the pot later. I made a corn salad and a fruit-and-yogurt dessert and put them in the refrigerator to chill.

Sissy and Mindi arrived at about four o'clock. The temperatures had stretched to reach thirty-seven degrees and, with the clear sunny skies, made it almost feel like spring. The eaves were shedding their icicles in rivulets. The snow hunkered down into a moist pack, which Milagro rolled into snowmen. She would yell "Sic 'em, Duchess," and Duchess would hurl her body against the round bodies, her huge jowls snapping the head into tiny pieces.

Sergio was getting Fancy out to groom and, I assumed, to ride with Sissy and Mindi as well as give her some exercise. I subtly shook my head no and jutted my chin toward the grain room. He rehooked the stall guard and followed me.

"Let them on their own today, Sergio. Stay close in case they need help, but let's build some confidence and independence today."

"Si," he answered with an understanding smile.

"If Jeffrey and JC come, you can pony Cloud next to Fancy."

"JC will like that. It will make him feel more in control."

"Right," I affirmed as I headed back to the house.

Doug arrived a little later. Duchess's bark alerted me that we had a new arrival. I grabbed a coat and slung it on as I charged out the door. He saw me coming and waited smiling. As I caught up to him, I put my arm about his waist, and he encircled me with his.

"I'm inviting Jeffrey and JC for dinner if they come this evening. Would you care to join us?"

"Most definitely. And if they don't come?"

"You're still invited."

"Do you want me to drive over to see if Jeffrey needs support?"

"You know Emma died?"

"Not until the funeral was over. My papers pile up until I have time to read them. I was going to tell you when I saw you again."

"Do you know where they live?"

"I think so. We left at the same time once, and I was behind them right to what I'm assuming is their place."

"Far from here?"

"Nope, just down the road."

Out of the corner of my eye, I saw Duchess charge down the lane about the same time my brain registered the sound of the school bus. I always got a kick out of how she sprang joyously as Joaquin got off the bus. To my surprise, Cindy also got off. I couldn't be sure, but she didn't seem very happy. I saw Duchess tackle her from behind. Her knees buckled, and she landed face-first in the plowed snow pile by the lane. Normally, she would have laughed and thrown a snowball for Duchess to catch in her mouth. But she just lay there. Duchess lay beside her, and I saw Cindy roll over, hug her, and bury her own face in the thick black fur of Duchess's neck. Joaquin knelt beside them and was quiet.

Doug turned to see what I was watching. It wasn't long before they all rose, and as Duchess bounced along beside them, Cindy and Joaquin ran and then slid on the smooth, packed snow of the lane. When she saw us, she smiled and waved, but the knot in my heart didn't go away.

When she drew near, I gave her a hug and said, "I'm so glad to see you."

She buried her face and hugged me fiercely. "I'm so ashamed I've neglected Fancy."

"We've been keeping her exercised. I'll bet she'll be glad to see you. Want to stay for dinner? Doug is staying, and I hope Jeffrey and JC also, if they come tonight."

"Maybe I should go then."

"No way, young lady. You can do your homework until it's time to leave. We'll clear it with your parents," exclaimed Doug.

She grinned a real smile then and said, "Thanks."

We all turned at the sound of Jeffrey's car motoring up the lane.

"We'd better get busy," announced Doug. He and Sergio headed for the stalls.

From where I was standing, the car looked crowded; and when it stopped, all four doors popped open. Jeffrey emerged visibly shaken. Little Chelsea Davis emerged with a huge smile on her face. JC came around the back of the car. He looked teary, and one cheek was bright red. Ted Davis threw his arm over JC's shoulder and pasted a sloppy grin on his face. Gone was the sullenness I'd seen before Thanksgiving.

"Jillian, I don't think we should stay." Jeffrey's voice was distraught.

"You've made it this far. Come spend time with Buck. He'll calm you."

I saw a flicker of hope cross his face, but it died quickly as he barely whispered, "I hurt JC. I'm sorry. I was just so overwhelmed, and his impatience set me off."

"Go spend time with Buck," I whispered back.

He went, and I turned to his son. "JC, it's good to see you. Who's your friend?"

"Cousin," he half sobbed.

I looked at Ted and saw him slightly lift his left hand in a wave at Cindy. Out of the corner of my eye, I saw Cindy, beet red, turn and run to the stall row. It appeared that feelings were flying around like sparks in an electrical short.

"Cousins?" I asked, looking at Ted.

"Yeah. Uncle Jeff married my aunt Peggy a gazillion years ago. Then she ran off. Grandma Rawling was helping them, but she died, so me and Chelsea are gonna help. Right, JC?"

JC nodded his head.

"Wow. This is neat. JC actually rides?"

"Can we ride too?" squealed the little girl.

"Chelsea," scolded Ted.

"JC, would you like to let Chelsea ride behind you?"

JC hesitated and then nodded.

"Or she can have a turn after you're done."

"She can ride behind me."

"What about Ted? Can he have a turn?" asked the concerned sister.

"Naw. That's okay."

I wondered if he was afraid of horses or trying not to be a bother. We'd soon find out.

Jeffrey didn't want to ride but was grooming Buck. Sergio had relinquished Fancy to Cindy and was walking Cloud with JC and

Chelsea aboard. JC sat up straight and looked proud to be sharing with the little girl who had her arms tightly vised around his body.

As I left the arena and went back into the stall row, I heard Ted talking to Cindy, who was saddling Fancy.

"I won't tell anyone, Cindy."

"Everyone knows!"

"Just at school. I won't tell any grown-ups."

I tried to act like I hadn't heard anything as I came in the door.

"Ted, how about learning how to groom? I'll let you work on Nanny."

As I was getting Nanny's grooming equipment, I heard Joaquin join our group. He got Nanny from her stall and put her in the crossties. When I set the equipment close by, I asked Joaquin if he would like to teach Ted about grooming.

"And then maybe you could take him for a ride as well."

That left me free to bring Hobbit out of her stall for a grooming.

Ted exclaimed, "Whoa, is she big."

"Yes, she is. Hobbit is my special buddy. No one rides her but me."

"That's okay by me."

"Ted, pay attention," scolded Joaquin. "You can't play around horses. They can really hurt you even accidentally. You should never stand right in front or right behind them. That's their blind spots."

I smiled as the little instructor continued his lecture.

CHAPTER TWENTY-FIVE

Life settled into a routine of barn work, bombproofing the horses, and pleasure riding. Classes resumed for me. The other nights, I tried to be in the barn when Doug showed up. I decided that instead of avoiding him, I wanted to get to know him, the better to choose if I wanted him as a permanent part of my life.

The Rawlings were a fixture on Thursday evenings. Doug seemed to have off Thursdays and was there to help with the novices. He took over instructing Jeffrey's lessons. Cindy took over Ted's equine education. Sergio and I guided JC and Chelsea. When I noticed Sissy was ready for new instruction, I had given her something else to work on.

I had noticed that Cindy was coming at least twice during the week and helped a lot with barn work on the weekends again. I couldn't help but wonder what had happened with the friendship with Tatum. And I kept a close eye on Ted when he was around Cindy. If she had been dropped by Tatum, I was afraid she'd try to find comfort with a preacher's son trying to prove he wasn't a good boy.

All seemed to be going smoothly until the Reverend Davis followed the Rawlings' car one Thursday evening. He was very irate that Ted and Chelsea had been riding without his consent for such a dangerous activity.

"Oh come on, Aaron," interrupted Jeffrey. "I'm here with them."

"And *that's* supposed to make me feel better?"

Jeffrey's face went blank, and then he turned and went back to Buck.

"That was cruel," I hissed, trying to keep my volume low. "I'm sorry. I should have thought to consult you, but I'd trust him with my kids."

"Do you have kids, Ms. Debaum?"

"No," I answered sheepishly.

"Then you have no idea what you're talking about. Jeffrey has been known to lose control."

"Not ever have I seen him lose control here. They're all happy here. The horses are a good family activity."

"Perhaps I could overlook this slip in judgment."

He gave me a look as he waited for me to interpret his meaning.

"You would take away a pleasure . . . a harmless pleasure from your children because I won't go out with you?"

His face darkened. "Is that your answer?"

"You didn't answer me," I persisted. I wanted him to say it out loud, to hear how petty it sounded.

As we stared each other down, Doug came over, put his arm around my waist, and asked, "Is there something I can help with?"

The preacher's eyes shifted to Doug's smiling face. "KIDS! LET'S GO!"

Chelsea was already by her father's side. She tugged his suited arm. "Daddy, please. The horses are fun."

"Get in the car," he said through gritted teeth, still staring at me.

"Daddy, nooooo."

Ted grabbed Chelsea and swung her up on his hip to carry her to the car. I saw him whisper in her ear and then try to put a gloved hand over her mouth to stifle her screams. JC was watching from Cloud's back. His face was growing red, his mouth contorting into a cry of his own. When Aaron followed his children to their car, JC slid from Cloud's back and slowly went to his father, softly calling "Dad?" as though uncertain of his reception.

Jeffrey turned toward him and held out his arms. JC rushed into them. "It's okay, JC. We're still okay. We'll be okay."

Doug leaned close. "Did I make matters worse?"

"No. Thanks for the support."

"It was selfish. I wanted him to know you were spoken for and to quit nagging you about going out with him."

I smiled up at him. "I appreciate that."

"Really?'

"Really."

He leaned down and kissed me softly on my lips. I felt myself starting to melt until I heard JC giggle and whisper, "Dad, look."

"Go ride Cloud, JC," said Jeffrey.

"Yeah, JC," I added, with my face still upturned to Doug. "Go ride Cloud."

—

In mid-February, I helped Doug move into his new apartment. It was small and sparse. The new clinic opened as well with a new partner. They had advertised the new clinic, and their first day was scheduled full, and many people came just for a look. For their open house, the waiting room was decorated with long balloons twisted into animal shapes. I had made animal cutout sugar cookies, a candy called Reindeer Doo, and a snack mix called Dog Chow. Madison provided homemade dog biscuits and cat treats. Free small bottles of a citrus pet shampoo were given out, and everyone could fill out a raffle ticket for a free grooming session for their pet at a local kennel. I had also made chicken salad sandwiches and homemade beef vegetable soup for Doug and his new partner, Destiny Jerue, and other members of the staff.

Destiny was a knockout, or so I thought. Her brunette hair was shaped in a pixie cut. Her eyes were a deep green; her teeth were white and even; her body was lean and muscular. I felt intimidated. Would Doug still want me after working in such close proximity with such beauty? I felt myself want to withdraw and sulk, but I forced myself to smile, shake her hand, and say "Pleased to meet you" even if it wasn't true. And then I headed home to sulk.

With the opening of the clinic's new branch, Doug immediately quit coming to visit Taz as often. *She moves fast.* I cried into my pillow at night. However, one night, it wasn't enough for Duchess to be licking my tears away. I needed a hug from Hobbit. I was surprised to see Doug's truck in the parking lot. I slid the door back, and in the lighted stall row stood Taz in crossties with Doug brushing him. He had looked up at the sound of the door rolling on the tracks. Even with his coat on, I thought he looked thinner.

"Hey, beautiful."

I couldn't help but smile. "Hey yourself."

"I've missed you."

"Really? You haven't dumped me then . . . or maybe you have?"

Shock registered on his face. "Well, I've gone from a four-man team down to a two-man team, so work has been taking a lot of time. Frankly, we didn't expect to be so busy. We've even run out of medical supplies. Madison and Gage have both made emergency trips with things. Sometimes I get out here pretty late, but why would you think I'd dump you?"

"Destiny is young and very pretty."

He grinned mischievously. "That she is. And you pictured us having hot sex on the exam table or back in the kennels?"

"No, but I probably will now."

"Well, don't. She may be young and pretty, but she isn't you. It has taken me all my life to find you. I'm not going to throw us away on a superficial fling."

"What if it turns out to not be a superficial fling?"

"Then I'd be awfully superficial. I promise, as soon as I can schedule myself a day off, I'll come spend it with you."

"I'll look forward to that."

"I have to warn you, however, if Destiny gets overwhelmed or any emergencies come up, I'll have to go."

"I understand. Do you think things will calm down soon?"

"If they don't, Madison has promised to hire another vet. She's going through applications now, going to start interviewing so she can hire fast if she needs to. But it could be another two to four weeks before she decides we're busy enough to take action." He chuckled. "I hope we last that long. We seldom have time to eat, and we've laughed about how much weight we've lost."

"I thought you looked thinner."

"Am I buff yet?"

"You always were."

"Thanks, by the way, for taking care of Taz. He always looks well-groomed and calm, so someone must be exercising and grooming him."

"We didn't know how you felt about someone riding him, so we've just been lunging him."

"I trust you, Sergio, and Cindy. I've seen you all ride."

"Okay, but what if you want to ride later?"

"He's a strong horse. Actually, he needs a lot of activity to keep him feeling his best. Coming as late as I have been, I've only been able to ride maybe a half hour. He'll feel better if someone else is supplementing that." He reached for me. "Want to have hot sex in the feed room?"

⟶

I started watching for Doug every night. I kept a folding chair and TV table set up in the stall row and soup or stew hot on the stove. I was soon tired from staying up, and there were nights that he looked totally beat as well.

"Sit. Eat. I'll groom. You can pick his hooves after you ride. He knows you're here."

"You're the best."

"Should I bring something to the clinic for you and Destiny? Will you have a chance to grab a bite if it's right there?"

"That would be awfully sweet of you."

Then one day, on my food run, there he was: Eric Sauceda— new grad, new vet, new partner. I could see the relief on Doug's and Destiny's faces. He was quite an asset, a real self-motivated go-getter. It would still be a few weeks while Eric learned the neighborhoods for the farm calls and the office routine. But there was light at the end of the tunnel.

It was then that I realized bare ground was showing in the sunny spots and the piles of snow that remained looked saggy and dismal and covered in dirt. It was a Saturday. The lot was full of familiar cars, and I was headed for the arena. The snowy owl swooped in front of me and then flew away to the north. For some reason, I stood transfixed and watched her until she was out of sight. *She's going home at last*, I thought as I continued toward the stall row.

To my surprise, the arena had the long-neglected obstacles set around—the mattresses, tarps, flags, and radio. There were waves and called greetings as though we hadn't seen one another for a long time. I realized I had been so wrapped up in the long hours with Doug and Destiny that I had missed out on many of their visits.

I was stunned to see Jeffrey, JC, Ted, and Chelsea there.

"Am I going to get a nasty message from your dad?" I asked them.

"No. He said he called you and left a message," Jeffrey announced.

"My gosh, I haven't even checked my answering machine."

"You've been preoccupied," said Cindy with a grin.

"So have schedules shifted, Jeffrey? Have you found a job?"

"Part-time, but we also still come on Thursdays if possible. Sergio said it would be okay. I hope it is."

"Absolutely. You're riding with more confidence. Sissy, same to you."

"Cindy has been giving me lessons."

"Good for her. I'd better go get my horse."

"Yes, you'd better," they cheered.

CHAPTER TWENTY-SIX

Spring was here at last. Crocuses, daffodils, hyacinths, and tulips marched out in ordered procession, their cheerful colors proclaiming renewed life. The rains and sun played leapfrog. Migrating birds passed through, and then some chose to stay.

One day, I watched a red-tailed hawk soar overhead and suddenly realized I hadn't seen the snowy owl since the day I had stood and watched her fly out of sight thinking she was at last headed home. I mused if it coincided with realizing I could shape-shift into who and what I wanted to be or if it was a coincidence.

As Joaquin and Milagro were outside more often to play, I wondered where their caregiver was, so one day, I asked Milagro.

"She got homesick, so she went home," explained the little girl.

What I couldn't explain was why the hair on my arms stood on end. And despite being told she was no longer there, I kept watching for those familiar wings in the sky and listening for a thud on my window.

It was nearing the one-year anniversary of attaining my dream, and I planned a small celebration. I invited all the veterinarians at Madison's two clinics, Gage, and all the people who came to share the dream with me. Mrs. Ley was the only one who RSVPed a refusal. Cindy's grades had dropped the past six weeks.

"Mrs. Ley, perhaps it isn't coming here that caused that."

"I'm aware of that, but it's all I have to use as leverage."

"Please don't. Give her friends a chance to help get her grades back up. I promise you she will pass with flying colors."

She hesitated only a moment. "Okay."

Cindy was to come to my place every evening after school where Doug or I would grill her in subjects after some time with the horses. Destiny even offered her knowledge in English and Spanish, which gave us a clue to her hidden talents.

It wasn't long before Cindy was caught up, studying for finals and keeping up with the class. We even inspired her to do an extra paper in her worst subject, history.

As often as Destiny came to tutor Cindy in languages, she never went near the barn. I had to ask her about it.

"Cats are more my style" was her answer.

"Really? What is it about cats that attracts you?"

"Their self-sufficiency, their balance, their aloofness. I guess I see myself that way."

"Do you have a lot of them?"

She laughed. "I'm not a crazy cat lady yet. I only have two, so they keep each other company during my long hours. But when I retire, I want to have a cat rescue."

"That's certainly a pressing need. How did you get so fluent in Spanish?"

"We lived along the border when I was young."

"And in English? I would have thought math and science were your strong suits."

"I had to work hard in math and science. My real love was English, literature, and writing."

"Then why become a vet?"

"I love animals too. I didn't have many friends growing up. Animals filled that need. I'm just giving back."

"But maybe you could have done a rescue on the side as giving back."

"No. I do the writing on the side . . . until I retire. Then I'll try to write full-time."

I felt a surge of jealousy, thinking of my own beleaguered writing. "Are you published?"

"No."

"Could I read some of your material?"

"Sure. I'll bring one the next time I come. Do you just want a short story or a novel?"

I gasped. "You have a novel written?"

"Working on my second novel, and I have a huge collection of short stories as well."

—

The weather wasn't as cooperative as the previous spring when I had moved in. This year, it was chillier and had rained all week. For my celebration party, we ended up inside with a small fire in the central pit to take the chill out of the room. I made barbecue ribs, three salads, two slaws, and peach and cherry pie à la modes.

I had set out a wide variety of games. Doug and Gage were battling it out over chess pieces. Connor, Eric, Ted, and Jeffrey were playing the dice game Bones. The kids were playing Go Fish. The majority were playing Scattergories. And a few sat off in a corner to exchange party chat. Duchess repeatedly made rounds to get tidbits from everyone's obliging fingers.

It was nine o'clock by the time the last guest had left. The party-chat group had left much earlier. Eric had left on an emergency farm call soon after the buffet.

Doug and Cindy had stayed to help me clean up. I set aside some leftovers for Cindy to take home. I gave her a hug and a kiss as she headed toward the door.

"Thank you so much for your help, Cindy. You are such a great friend."

She burst into tears.

I hugged her tight, and Doug came to join, wrapping his muscular arms around both of us.

"What's wrong, sweetie?"

"I'm not a good friend. I'm just a freak."

"Who says that?" bellowed Doug.

Cindy had to grin, but it disappeared as quickly as it had come. "Tatum." She started sobbing again. "And she screamed it in the cafeteria in front of everyone."

"It must have hurt to be betrayed like that."

"Don't you think I'm being a baby for letting it bother me?"

"It would sure bother me," I asserted.

"Me too," Doug assured her.

"Cindy, I know you want friends your own age, and I think you should keep trying, but I also think you're just too special for most kids. It must be hard having only adults to relate to. Ted's trying to be a friend, isn't he?"

"I think so, but I'm not sure."

"Well, don't be afraid to tell him to back off," chimed in Doug. "And if he gives you *any* problems, you let me know."

That brought a real smile to her face. She threw her arms around him. "Thanks, Doug."

The warm sunny days became more numerous. Everyone wanted to be outside. Sergio started preparing the garden plot for planting. I was kneeling in the flower gardens, loosening the soil and digging out clumps of grass. I had the house windows open to air out the stale winter atmosphere. I could hear the phone ring but figured that if it was important, they'd call back or leave a message. I was telling Sergio that I had plenty of frozen stuff from last year and so didn't think we needed to plant such a big garden. He countered that perhaps we could still plant and set up a produce stand to sell it. I told him that I wanted some fresh stuff but to go ahead. He could keep all the money they made. They could even pick the excess fruits to sell if he wanted.

Sergio helped me get the agility obstacles out of storage and set up. I walked Duchess through the course to see how much she remembered and again just to refresh her memory.

We were bringing in the horses when Joaquin and Cindy got off the bus. They went in to change their clothes, and by the time they got to the barn, Sissy and Mindi were pulling in the drive. Nobody wanted to ride in the arena, so we decided on a group trail ride. We were almost to the far side of the hayfield when we heard cantering hooves. Doug slowed Taz to a trot to approach us slowly so as to not encourage our mounts to run or frolic.

As we rounded the far side of the woods and were returning up the east side, we could tell the temperature was dropping. We hadn't gone any faster than a walk, so a quick brush and feed was all the horses needed.

The inside of the house was quite cool. Cindy, Doug, and I circulated through the rooms closing windows. Doug lit some kindling in the fire pit. I went to the kitchen to make ham-and-cheese sandwiches and hot soup. Cindy had put all her A papers on the kitchen table: Spanish, algebra, history, and English. I was just about to yell congratulations when Doug yelled, "You've got a message on your answering machine. Want me to play it back?'

"Sure."

We all listened as Madison asked if I was going to ride in or help with the spring trail ride. Instead of an answer, the first thing out of my mouth was "Oh my gosh. I promised Jeremiah I'd learn to dance."

Doug came through the door with a grin on his ruggedly handsome face. "You are in luck. I'm a great dancer. I'll teach you. We'll have our first lesson tonight."

"I don't know. Cindy might laugh at me."

Cindy giggled. "Probably will, but that's too bad."

"Well, you can have a lesson also, unless you already know how to dance. And by the way, those As are very impressive."

"Thanks to my friends. So are you gonna help or ride?"

"I think I'd prefer to ride in the fall, so I'll help. That'll give the horses a lot more time to build up muscle before we ask so much of them."

"Then I'll help also and ride in the fall," chimed in Doug.

"Cindy, do you think Fancy will be ready to ride by the fall? If so, you can ride her in the trail ride then."

"Oh my gosh. I'm finally going to get to ride my own horse in the trail ride." She stopped and reddened. "Well, not actually mine."

"Yes, Cindy. Yours for as long as you can care for her." I turned to Doug. "Do you think you'll be able to get that night off?"

"No problem. Destiny already said she'd work for both trail rides so Eric and I can participate."

"Does Eric have a horse?"

"No, but he grew up on the reservation and has riding experience. But he might just help at the fires."

"And how nice of Destiny to cover for you, which reminds me—did you know she's a writer on the side?"

"No."

"I'm reading the manuscript of her first novel. I think it's really good. I wish I could help her get it published."

"That good, huh?"

"I think so, but what do I know?"

"I know a writer," enthused Cindy. "Maybe she can help."

"Let's be sure to ask Destiny if she wants to try to publish the next time we see her. Guess I'd better call Madison and let her know she has three helpers and see what she needs. Someone stir the soup."

CHAPTER TWENTY-SEVEN

I was sitting in evening shade. The birds were coming in from their daily work to bathe and roost. Sergio, Jeffrey, Doug, Gage, and Gage's son, Garrett, were putting the last bales of the first-cutting hay on the wagon that still needed to make the twenty-mile trip to Madison's Lucky Deuces farm. I didn't envy Gage that trip. It would be a late night for him. But a roast was ready to refuel his system after all-day baling and stacking forty-pound rectangles of sweet-smelling grass hay before he started out. I had a thermos of coffee ready to go with him as the temperatures were supposed to drop.

They threw the last few bales up on the wagon and headed for the buckets of warm, soapy water and clean T-shirts I had had made. The shirts sported the words "I baled at Jillian's." I had grinned as I laid them out for them and then headed inside to throw the salad together. I heard the rumble of the tractor as it came from the field and was parked in the drive ready to take the last leg of the journey. I couldn't help but look out the window at the manly, bare backs as they washed off sweat and bits of itchy hay. They toweled their muscles dry and slipped on the fresh clothes, laughing in camaraderie and at the new shirts.

That's my guy, I thought to myself as I glanced down at the diamond on my finger to be sure it was still there. It wasn't a dream. Doug had put me into a twirl while dancing on the spring trail ride and pulled me back into his chest where one arm held me and the other presented me with the ring while whispering in my ear, "Will you marry me?"

So easily the yes flowed from my mouth. No qualms, only elation.

Cindy was drawn to the stables at the spring trail ride where a sad old gray was up for sale. The owner was selling because Admiral of the Fleet was thirty years old and, with arthritic joints, had lost his finesse in the dance of dressage. He just wasn't good enough anymore. So the big gelding was now in my stall row providing a dressage mount for Cindy to take lessons on. Her family decided they would pay for the lessons and had engaged Arielle to come give them once a week.

My guy, my dream, my magic horses, I thought. I poked my arm and knocked on the countertop as if to test their reality. I felt my life was full and satisfying as it had never been before. I had come full circle—from having a dream to acquiring it, from a solitary life to one full of horses and friends, from being focused on my goals to helping others achieve theirs.

Jeffrey was getting help with his PTSD and holding a job, comforting and getting comfort from Buck. Destiny had found a literary agent through Cindy's friend Jewell Fitzgerald. Elena had graduated third in her class of LPNs, had a job at a nursing home in Clear Point, and planned to go for her RN after Sergio finished his schooling. Sergio was signed up to start welding classes in the autumn. All the horses were thriving. There was still much to do. The equine supply store was only partially built; Doug and I had discussed building an additional stall row with another eight stalls. We were going to make the first stall on the left to be the foyer to the new stall wing. An additional pasture needed to be fenced in.

Only the death of Duchess marred the journey. She was flying through the air, over a jump in the agility course, when her heart just stopped. She was dead before she hit the ground. I grieved for my dear friend, but Doug assured me she had been happy with me and with soaring through the air at the time her spirit departed. Cindy agreed. But I still miss my friend.

My thoughts rested on Hobbit, and I saw her in the pasture lifting her head from grazing to look in the direction of the house.

What People Are Saying about *Hoof Beats*

Hoof Beats draws you into the story from the start. The characters come to life as you get drawn into their lives; empathizing with them in the sad times, cheering them on in the good. Once I started reading it was hard to put down. By the end I was already looking forward to the next book. (Bev Emerick, Massillon, Ohio)

What People Are Saying about *Horse Power*

Horse Power by Rae D'Arcy is a warmhearted novel. We accompany the leading character on a developmental journey full of suspense. I love this book. (Margit Roth, Hagen, Germany)

Jillian has spent her whole working life preparing to have an equine rescue farm as a retirement avocation. At last, she is standing on her farm, her body aching, worn-down, alone. But the need for foster homes is great, and as Jillian plows ahead to take in the horses that need her, the magic begins.

Printed in the United States
By Bookmasters